Love on Trial

DIANA PALMER

Published by Silhouette Books
America's Publisher of Contemporary Romance

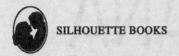 **SILHOUETTE BOOKS**

ISBN 0-373-51207-4

LOVE ON TRIAL

First published in North America as a MacFadden Romance by Kim Publishing Corporation.

Copyright © 1979 by Diana Palmer.

Visit Silhouette at www.eHarlequin.com

Printed in U.S.A.

One

The little coffee shop was crowded, its spotless white linen tablecloths and tempting aromas drawing a maximum crowd, but the two stubborn young women weren't discouraged. They managed to find one empty table and collapsed into the dainty chairs, spilling their packages onto the floor with weary sighs.

"I thought you said the stores would

all be empty on a day this hot,'' Marty reminded her friend with a glare over the single rose in its ceramic budvase.

The slender young blonde only smiled, her amber eyes sparkling. ''I didn't say empty of what,'' she laughed.

''Oh, Siri,'' her friend moaned, ''you're just impossible!''

Cyrene Jamesson studied the over-sized menu with silent amusement, warming to the sound of her nickname. No one called her Cyrene except Mark; but, then, her conservative-minded boyfriend never called anyone by a nickname.

She put the menu aside after making an instant decision, and watched Marty frown uncertainly over the varieties of coffee and pastries.

''Why not close your eyes and point at one?'' Siri suggested helpfully.

''That's easy for you to say,'' came the reply. ''You don't have to watch your weight.''

She sighed. "At the speed I move, it's impossible to gain weight."

"You didn't have to be a reporter, you know," Marty reminded her.

Siri looked thunderstruck. "You mean," she said in mock astonishment, "there are other professions that cater to crazy people?"

"You're not crazy."

"No," Siri agreed. "Most people run river races in inner tubes, hang out of airplanes with 35 mm cameras, lie down behind cars while police tear-gas snipers, and chase bank robbers down back streets."

Marty closed her eyes. "Deliver me," she whispered.

Seconds later, a young, harried waitress darted toward them with her order book in hand, almost panting with the effort. "Sorry I took so long," she apologized. "We're swamped today!"

"Only because the coffee's so good." Siri smiled.

The waitress beamed and took their order, darting off again in a flurry of ruffled apron.

"Miss Diplomacy strikes again," Marty laughed, tossing her dark hair.

"It doesn't cost anything to be nice to people," Siri reminded her.

"Reporters are supposed to be hard, uncompromising and stubborn," Marty remarked. "Aren't they?"

"That's only a stereotype. You can't lump people into groups and label them anymore, it's too complicated."

"Thanks for the benefit of that priceless bit of wisdom from Psychology 102," Marty laughed.

"Wait till we get the pastries and coffee," Siri threatened, "and I'll treat you to a lecture on Glasser's theories."

"Please, we don't all share your fascination with abnormal psychology," came a moan from the other side of the table. "How does your poor old Dad stand it?"

"He likes it."

"He would," Marty grumbled. "Does Hawke?"

The light went out of Siri's rosy complexioned face.

"Don't mention that savage to me," Siri growled.

"Siri, what's wrong with you?" her friend wondered. "Half the women in the country would give their eye-teeth just to meet that gorgeous man. And there he is, your father's partner, one of the most famous criminal lawyers alive, and you don't even like him!"

"Hawke doesn't go out of his way to be likeable," she replied quietly. "He thinks all women should be locked up in harems and only let out once a year to have their hair trimmed."

"While you, my dotty friend, are the world's foremost libber."

"Guilty as charged." Siri smiled. "Hawke's too *macho* for my taste. We've always knocked sparks from each other, ever since Dad took him on seven years ago.''

''Not all the time, though.'' Marty grinned. ''I've seen a few pictures of the two of you together at parties.''

''He can be pleasant enough. There are times when I feel almost comfortable with him. And the very next minute, he'll say something to get my back up and laugh when I lose my temper.'' Siri shook her head. ''It's never dull, I'll give you that.''

Siri got a brief respite while the waitress set two cups of *Kaffee mit Schlag* in dainty wineglasses before them, along with delicate French cream cakes.

''Two thousand calories a bite,'' Marty moaned.

''Only,'' Siri remarked, ''if you eat it. Why not just sit there and gaze at it lovingly?''

Marty glared at her and dug into the cream cake with a vengeance.

''That was delightful,'' Siri sighed as

she finished the last drop of her strong coffee. "This is the best day off I've had in months."

"Naturally. It's the only day off you've had in months. How did you manage it?"

Siri laughed. "Because of the Devolg murder case."

Marty blinked at her. "Huh?"

"You've heard of it? The young boy who was accused of the knife murder of Justin Devolg?"

The brunette's mouth flew open. "You mean the case that's been on the front page…"

"The same. Hawke's counsel for the defense," she added.

"I still don't get it. Why did that get you a day off?"

"Because," Siri said calmly, "Bill Daeton wants me to go to Panama City with Hawke to track down a witness in the case."

"Oh, you lucky little devil." Marty

smiled. "Panama City, all expenses paid, and Hawke Grayson!"

"Hold it right there. I said Bill wants me to go, not that I plan to do it."

Marty lifted her eyes. "And why, pray tell, aren't you going? Doesn't Hawke want you along?"

"You're getting warmer. Bill asked Dad to approach him about it," Siri explained, "because he knew I'd refuse. So Dad asked him."

Marty leaned forward earnestly, moving the budvase aside. "So?"

"Hawke told Dad he had enough to do without playing chaperone to an adolescent."

"Adolescent! Siri, you're twenty-one years old!"

"To a man of Hawke's advanced years," the blonde said maliciously, "I probably do seem underaged."

"I thought he was in his middle thirties."

"Late thirties," Siri corrected, "or

early forties. I've never asked. He's too old for me, and that's a fact. Anyway, he said it was fine if Bill wanted to send a male reporter along, as long as Hawke had some control over the story to make sure the facts were presented accurately. How do you like that? A male reporter was welcome, but I can go hang.''

"What did Bill say?"

"I don't know, I haven't asked him." She fished in her purse for a five dollar bill. "Hawke really burns me up. It isn't that I wanted to have to go with him, it's just the principle of the thing. I guess it's just as well, though, you know how Mark is.''

"Don't I just?" Marty said venomously. "That pompous little...!"

"Now, Marty."

"Don't you 'now, Marty' me!" the other girl grumbled. "Why you put up with him is beyond me."

"Because he's good company most of the time, and he doesn't make demands,''

Siri said quietly. "I don't have to fight him off, and we do enjoy each other's company."

"How exciting!"

"I don't want excitement in my private life," Siri said. "I get enough of that during the day running from fires to murder scenes."

"I'm waiting," Marty said.

"For what?"

"For that old 'eyes and ears' of John Q. Public routine," she laughed. "Honestly, Siri, I think you bleed ink!"

"Of course!" she replied with a smile. "It's required."

She took the Marta bus to the corner of Peachtree and 10th Street, and got off there. It was such a pretty day, she felt like walking the rest of the way to her father's law office. She sighed, studying the Atlanta skyline, the new construction, and the mingling of old architecture with modern innovation. It was difficult to picture what this great city must have been like in 1864 when it was ravaged by Sherman's army. For an urban area, it was strangely small-townish. There was a community feeling among the people who lived in the old elegant apartment houses along the wide street, among the merchants who ran small shops there. Siri always felt comfortable in this stretch of the city, despite the alarming crime rate. Of course, she had the good sense not to venture out alone at night.

She turned into the office building where her father had his practice, and took the elevator to the 10th floor, which was occupied by the law firm of Jamesson, Grayson, Peafowler, Dinkham, and Guystetter.

Her father's middle-aged secretary, Nadine, greeted her with a smile.

"He's here," she said before Siri could ask. "Shall I warn him, or do you prefer to have the element of surprise?"

Siri smiled from ear to ear. She liked the trim, little brunette who was so like

her late mother. If only Jared Jamesson
would notice what a jewel of a woman
his secretary was...Siri shrugged mentally.

"I think it might be safer if you an-
nounce me," Siri told her with a wink.
"I'll know if I'm in the doghouse before
I walk in."

Nadine nodded and pressed the buzzer.
"Mr. Jamesson, your daughter's here to
see you. Shall I send her in?"

"You're mistaken, Miss Green," came
the deep, sharp reply, "I don't have a
daughter. My daughter wouldn't let herself be shoved aside from a juicy assignment like the Devolg murder case."

Siri leaned over the intercom. "She
would if Hawke Grayson has his way,"
she said into it. "You can't argue with a
brick wall, Papa dear."

There was a deep chuckle in the back-
ground, joined by her father's muffled
laugh.

"Come on in, Siri. I think I've convinced the brick wall for you."

Siri straightened with an apprehensive look at Nadine. "Is Hawke in there?" she asked with irritation.

"If I say yes, are you planning to dive for the elevator?" Nadine asked.

Siri shook her head. "I wouldn't give him the satisfaction," she replied. She straightened her shoulders and opened the door to her father's plush office.

Jared Jamesson was stretched back in the swivel chair behind his desk, with his elbows jutting out to either side behind his head. Hawke was perched on the edge of the big oak desk, looking, as usual, dark and formidable.

"Do you still want to go to Panama City?" Jared asked his daughter, swinging forward to rest his forearms flat on the desk.

Siri shrugged. "Not if it's going to mean giving up my bubble gum and my

Barbie doll,'' she said with a pointed glance in Hawke's direction.

She could see the tiny dark flames that began to smoulder in her target's eyes, as he folded his arms across his massive chest and raised an eyebrow. He didn't smile at the dig. But, then, Hawke almost never smiled.

''Someday, sparrow,'' he told her, ''I'm going to make up for a noticeable omission in your upbringing. Jared ruined you.''

She tossed her thick blond hair, making a face at the nickname. ''No, he didn't,'' she defended her parent, ''every good father gives his children champagne for lunch and takes them to girlie shows at night.''

''Siri!'' Jared burst out, horrified.

She laughed. ''It's okay, Dad, I didn't mean it. Hawke, we never had champagne for lunch; only for supper,'' she added, and ignored Jared's groan.

''No wonder your father's hair is

gray,'' Hawke remarked in that deep, resonant voice that carried so well in a courtroom. ''Well, do you want to go with me, or don't you?''

She didn't but she'd have died rather than admit it. She really wasn't prepared to find an explanation.

''I thought you hated reporters,'' she recalled. Her fingers tightened around the full shopping bag and her purse.

''Only certain unscrupulous ones,'' he corrected. ''In this case, if I give you an exclusive, at least I can be sure the facts you release are accurate. And,'' he added, reaching for a cigarette, ''you won't be able to print a word of it until I say so.''

''Or what?'' she challenged.

He lit the cigarette before he replied. ''I'll sue the hell out of your paper. And I'll win.''

That wasn't conceit. It was a statement of fact, just as if he'd made a comment on the weather, and she knew it. His deep, slow voice sent shivers down her spine.

"Does Bill Daeton know you get the final word on the release date on my copy?" she asked.

He blew out a cloud of smoke. "What do you think?"

She glanced toward her father, who was listening to the exchange with amusement sparkling in the amber eyes that his daughter had inherited from him.

"Do you want to go or not, Siri?" Hawke asked pointedly.

"Well, if I can get somebody to take my assignments for a few days," she mumbled. "I've got that interview with..."

"Excuses?" Hawke prodded. "Or is it that Holland doesn't approve?"

She bristled at the sarcastic reference to her boyfriend. "Mark does have some say in what I do."

"Why should he?" came the harsh reply. "Do you tell him how to do his job at the accounting agency, or where he can travel in connection with it?''

"You don't understand, Hawke...!''

"The hell I don't!'' he growled.

"Now, now, world tensions are bad enough without World War III erupting between you two,'' Jared remarked, moving to stand between them. "And I don't have time to referee.''

Siri and Hawke exchanged glares, but her eyes fell first. He always managed to back her down, and it burned her up inside that she yielded so easily.

"All right, I'll go home and pack,'' she grumbled, turning away.

"I won't be able to get away before Thursday,'' Hawke said coolly. "Criminal court's in session all week, and I've got two clients to represent. If the jury doesn't get deadlocked, I should be able to leave Friday morning. Check with me later in the week.''

She nodded. "See you at home, Dad,'' she called over her shoulder.

"Don't trip over your mouth on the way out," her parent called after her.

"You should have gone into comedy instead of court," she called back, and closed the door behind her with a flair.

"How'd it go?" Nadine asked as she headed toward the elevator.

Siri paused, thought for a minute, and smiled. "I lost."

"You have to stay home?"

Siri shook her head. "I have to go." She grinned.

The smile faded when she was in the elevator, alone, going down to street level. How in the world was she going to explain to Mark, who didn't trust her past his heel, that she was going away for a week with the most notorious man in local legal circles? From one battle to another, she thought resignedly. But at least with Mark, she'd have a chance of winning, which was more than she'd ever had with Hawke Grayson.

Two

Siri fumed around the house like a steaming clam, and every time she saw that arrogant dark head, she fumed even more. The trouble with Hawke, she told herself, was that he was too used to feminine adulation. He was accustomed to getting his own way about everything. But, even so...why did she always yield?

"He makes me feel like a spoiled brat," she grumbled, as she headed for the shower. "That's why I don't like him!"

Not that she was spoiled. Jared had seen to that. When her mother died, just before Siri's sixth birthday, he'd made sure she had enough love to make up for both parents. But he hadn't indulged her to any great extent. His law practice took up a great deal of his time, and Siri had to settle for odd moments of togetherness. Jared didn't spoil her; he forced her to fight her battles on all fronts. Even now, he only interfered when things got blazing hot between Hawke and his daughter. Which was another curious thing, Siri thought as she undressed and stepped under the spray of warm water.

She wasn't naturally antagonistic toward anyone, except her father's famous partner. It had been that way from the beginning, as if she'd sensed in Hawke an adversary the first time she saw him. There had been the occasional pleasant time, as Marty had hinted earlier. But even those fleeting moments of affinity had been laced with tension, because she could never relax completely with Hawke. No matter how congenial he was on the surface, she always felt the tingle of deep fires burning just under his impassive exterior.

She stepped out of the shower refreshed, and was on her way to change when the phone caught her.

"County morgue," she droned into the receiver, expecting to hear Marty's voice on the other end.

There was a brief pause, followed by an irritated masculine sigh. "Must you answer the phone that way, Cyrene? What if it had been mother, or your editor?"

She raised her eyes heavenward. "Mark," she explained patiently, "I'm a reporter, remember? This is the way I am."

"So you keep telling me. Never mind.

We're having dinner at the Magnolia Inn. I'll pick you up at six."

"I know," she reminded him. "You told me yesterday."

"Yes," he said in a long-suffering tone. "But you tend to forget dates you make with me as you move from fire to murder."

"It was only once," she defended herself. "And you know it was one of the very biggest fires in the city."

"And that's another thing," he grumbled, "always hanging around with men; firemen, policemen, civil defense..."

"It's my job, Mark," she reminded him.

"But, Siri, the way it looks..."

Her temper boiled over. "That's it," she said tightly, "if you can't bring yourself to accept me the way I am, you can jolly well go chase yourself!" With that, she slammed the receiver down.

She didn't get two steps before the

phone rang again. She jerked it up. "Yes?" she asked impatiently.

"I'm sorry," he said. "It's been a long day, and I'm in a rotten mood. Come out with me and cheer me up."

Out of habit, or weariness, she gave in. After all, she wasn't any more perfect than he was.

They went to a popular restaurant on the outskirts of the city, and business was booming.

Without bothering to ask if the cigarette smoke would bother her, Mark led her straight to the smoking section of the plush, carpeted restaurant and seated her. She barely had time to scan the extensive and appetizing menu before the waitress was asking for her order. She ordered a steak, wild rice and a tossed salad bypassing the delicious but horribly fattening strawberry shortcake with its foot-high topping of whipped cream. The waitress returned a few moments later with trays laden with steaming, fragrant dishes.

She thanked the girl—who looked as if she could press 200 pounds without any effort from the way she was handling those heavy trays—and froze as she looked past the girl's frilly apron.

Hawke and his current girlfriend, a darkly elegant brunette in a dress cut almost to the waist, were seated just across the way. Siri carefully rearranged her chair so that her back was slightly toward them, and hoped Hawke wouldn't notice her.

"It's been a rotten day," Mark sighed as he attacked his steak. "One of my clients had to go downtown for an audit with the tax people, and they found a mistake. My secretary," he groaned, "typed the right numbers, but in the wrong places. So instead of getting the refund he expected, my client wound up owing money."

"How awful," Siri said automatically.

"Amen. I caught it from both sides." He reached for his soft drink, grimacing at the steaming cup of black coffee at Siri's right. "How can you drink that stuff?"

She shrugged. "Habit, I guess. Dad and I always have it for breakfast and dinner—with every meal."

There was the sudden interruption of loud conversation just behind her, and she caught the familiar sound of a rival reporter's voice.

"I hear there's some new evidence in the Devolg case, Mr. Grayson," Sandy Cudor was probing in his pleasant voice. "Anything to the rumors?"

"You'll find out in the courtroom, Sandy," came the deep, equally pleasant reply.

"In other words, you aren't talking," the reporter interpreted, and Siri knew there would be a smile on the young man's face.

"Exactly."

"Well, have a nice evening," Sandy said, and Siri instinctively leaned down to pick up the napkin she dropped on purpose, so that her colleague wouldn't see her. It worked.

"Disgusting," Mark was grumbling.

"What is?" she asked.

"Reporters," he replied with a glare after Cudor's retreating back. "And grandstanding lawyers," he added for a good measure.

"Just hold it right there," she told him icily. "If there's any grandstanding, it's usually done by young lawyers trying to make reputations. Hawke's a long way past the struggling stage. And Sandy may be impetuous, but he's young and learning, and bound to be a little overeager."

"I didn't think you cared a fig about either one of them," Mark recalled, his own voice cool.

"I don't," she agreed. "But then you aren't attacking personalities, you're attacking two professions that I know intimately.''

He drew a harsh sigh and tossed down the rest of his soft drink. "You don't even have to work," he said unpleasantly. "I don't know why you insist on pursuing that job—"

"Because I like it!" she shot back.

"You like associating with all those men, and showing your legs," he retorted.

"You go to hell," she said in a furious whisper, her amber eyes shooting flames toward him, as she crumpled her napkin and threw it down to the right side of her plate.

"I didn't think it was so easy to keep secrets in a newsroom," Hawke remarked from behind her.

She turned, flushed with anger, to meet the taunting light in his dark eyes as he paused beside their table with the impatient brunette on his arm.

"It isn't," Siri managed, irritated at

the breathless tone of her usually steady voice, hating the effect Hawke always had on her nerves. "I don't suppose Bill's told any of them yet."

"If he does, you'd better check under your hood every afternoon before you leave there," came the cool reply. "Hello, Holland," he added, finally acknowledging the younger man's presence.

"Hello," Mark grumbled. His eyes speared Siri. "What's all this about?"

"Siri hasn't told you?" Hawke asked, and even though he didn't smile, the mocking amusement was there in those unfathomable eyes. "She's going with me to Panama City for a week to research some new evidence in the Devolg case."

Mark's thin face flushed red. "Is she? It's new to me!" He glared at Siri. "Does your father know?"

"I'm twenty-one years old, almost twenty-two," she replied. "I don't need Daddy's permission!"

"My God, how am I going to explain it to mother?" he groaned.

"No dessert?" Hawke remarked, noticing Siri's barely touched dinner. "You're thin enough, aren't you?"

"She's just fine the way she is, thanks. I don't want her to look like a cow," Mark replied hotly, with a speaking glance at the well-endowed brunette beside Hawke, who bristled visibly at the insult.

Hawke didn't say anything, but his eyebrows went up as if the remark astonished him.

"Enjoy your dinner," Hawke said pleasantly, and escorted the brunette out of the spacious dining room.

"I don't like that man," Mark grumbled, glaring at the retreating broad back. "What business is it of his how you look or what you eat? And what the devil did he mean about you going with him to Panama City?"

"Just what he said," Siri replied

coolly. "You don't own me, Mark. Not now, not ever, and I can't think how you've convinced yourself that you did. I don't have to apologize to you for the job I do. And that's precisely what the trip concerns—my job. I won't be sharing Hawke's bed, if that's what you're wondering."

The way he averted his eyes told her what he'd thought.

"I should think you'd be too young to interest a man like that anyway," he finally said. "He must be at least forty."

That bothered her for some reason, but she bit her lip to keep from making a reply. "Hawke's got all the women he needs, I imagine," she said finally.

"I don't doubt it." He laughed humorlessly. "Wasn't his father a shipbuilder, or owned a fleet of ships or something in Charleston?"

"Something like that."

"And his mother was an heiress. There was some horrible scandal before he left there." Mark frowned, trying to remember.

"Was there? I don't keep tails on Hawke, I never have. He's Dad's partner, not mine, and I like it that way," she said harshly.

"If you dislike him so much," he protested, "why do you start changing color the minute you see him?"

"Do I?" She searched in her purse for her compact and lipstick. "Temper, probably. He's always telling me how inferior a woman reporter is, and this afternoon was no exception. Dad had to separate us."

There was a long pause while she put on her lipstick. "Siri, I'm sorry," he said finally. "It's just that I don't trust him around you. You're so...naive."

She almost laughed. Mark, who'd never even tried to touch her, or intimately kiss her, telling her she was naive.

"To Hawke, I'm still the teenager he used to bring to football games when I was a cheerleader. He doesn't think of me as a woman.'' And, boy, am I glad, she almost added. She'd never seen Hawke in action, but she'd have bet her typewriter that there wasn't a woman alive he couldn't get with that dark, sensual charm. She didn't really want to find out if she could resist it. Besides, she told herself silently, he was almost twice her age. Far too old to even dream about.

''Can we go now?'' Siri asked, putting away her cosmetics. ''I'm really tired.''

''Of course. Just let me finish this cigarette,'' he said, lighting one up. ''Won't be a minute.''

It was ten, and she felt like screaming before he finally stubbed it out and took her home.

''Siri, got a minute?'' Bill Daeton called from the doorway of his office.

She left the half-finished story on her desk and joined him. ''What's up?''

''Look, I know you don't do family

news," he said, anticipating an argument, "but I've got a great feature story on my desk and no cameraman to shoot it. Can you spare an hour from that burglary wrap-up to take some pictures of an art exhibit at the museum? There are a couple of paintings by Jacques Lavelle in it—you know, our local talent who does those exquisite portraits in pastels?"

She glared at him without speaking.

"Think of the class that story will give the paper," he coaxed, "an international exhibit, right here in our city, and a local artist included in it, along with some of the old masters. The arts council will love it. So will old Sumerson. Remember that? He owns 65% of the stock in our publishing company? Pays both our salaries? Siri, dammit, I haven't got a photog. Everyone's out on assignment, and I've got to have those shots today!"

She saw a chance for some bargaining and grinned. "Remember that opinion poll you wanted me to conduct in my

spare time to see how local people felt on
the gun control issue? Well, if you'll
make Sandy do it instead, I'll just be
purely tickled to cover your art exhibit!''

''Blackmailer!'' he burst out.

''It's no worse than what you did to
me,'' she replied. ''A week in Panama
City with Hawke Grayson…one or both
of us will be in shreds by the time we
come home, and it'll be all your fault.
You knew I didn't want to go.''

''Who else was there to send?''

She sighed. ''Do we have a deal?''

''Sandy,'' he reminded her, ''already
has it in for you. I told him this morning
about the Devolg case.''

''He's young,'' she said soothingly.
''He'll get over it. And if he won't, send
him instead!'' She grinned.

''Can't. I've already got him assigned
to the lottery investigation.''

''City editors,'' she said with vigor,
''were invented by God to torment the
ignorant.''

"Thanks." He grinned. "Now get out of here and get those pictures. And don't forget, I'm still searching for somebody to take over the 'Dear Mother Jones' column permanently."

"Sadist," she mumbled as she walked away.

The art exhibit was delightful to shoot. The lighting was good, the subject matter was fascinating, and, best of all, it got her out of the office. She sat down on one of the brocade benches, clutching the camera, and stared blankly at a charcoal sketch. The really wonderful thing about reporting was that it didn't tie you to a desk for eight hours. You could get out into the city, meet people, and visit exciting places, without having to belong to any elite crowd. It was always exciting, even a little dangerous at times. Most of the women she knew would rather have suffered torture than trade jobs with her. But she knew with a certainty, that she couldn't have endured being a secretary or a receptionist. She was only alive with a pad and pen and a camera in her hands.

"I might have known I'd find you here," Hawke said suddenly, and she whirled on the bench to find him leaning carelessly against one of the big round columns, his hands in his pockets, just watching her.

Her heart flew up in her chest, but it was just the unexpected surprise of seeing him, she told herself.

"I...Bill bribed me," she stammered.

"Did he have to twist your arm that hard?" he asked. "You love these damned things."

"Guilty," she admitted with a tiny smile, slinging her collar length blond hair away from her face. "But he didn't know that. I got out of doing an opinion poll."

"Witch. Sometimes I think you cast spells."

"So does Mark," she sighed. Her eyes

brushed the beauty of the canvasses on the high walls. "You got me into a devil of a mess last night. I was going to wait until he was in a better mood to break the news to him."

"I've never seen him in a good mood. He's a whiner, sparrow. The world's full of them...complainers without the guts to change the things they complain about."

"People can't help being what they are, Hawke," she said quietly, avoiding those piercing dark eyes. "You can't go around trying to change people to suit your own taste."

"At least your father taught you that," he replied. "Where do you go from here?"

"I thought I'd go steal bread crumbs from the pigeons in the park," she replied.

"You look like that's what you do for lunch every day," he said with an unappreciative glance at her slender figure. "Come on."

"Where are we going?" she asked, grasping her camera and purse as she tried to keep up with his long, quick strides.

"To Kebo's. I'm going to feed you."

She drew back. "Oh, no, not today. It's Wednesday," she told him.

"So, what the hell does that have to do with it?" he demanded, his face leonine and faintly dangerous.

"Middle of the week, and I owe my soul to a mechanic on Peachtree Street for repairs on the VW," she said in a breathless rush. "I simply can't afford Kebo's. You'll have to take me to the Krystal instead."

His eyes narrowed, and his square jaw locked stubbornly. "You damned little independent mule," he growled softly. "I said I was taking you to lunch, and I can afford Kebo's. Now come on."

"Yes, sir!" she replied smartly, and had to skip to keep up with him.

It wasn't until they were inside the

plush restaurant enjoying roast beef au jus and perfectly cooked scalloped potatoes with a salad, that she began to wonder how Hawke had known where to find her.

"I wasn't looking for you," he replied when she asked the question. "I stopped by to see Lavelle's part of the exhibit. I represented him in a libel case several years ago. His art impressed me then. It still does."

"It's surrealistic," Siri commented.

One dark, heavy eyebrow went up. "Yes, it is."

Her lower lip pouted as she added a touch of the thick cream to her coffee and stirred it. "I'm not completely ignorant when it comes to things like art."

"I never said you were. I thought your taste ran to Renoir and Degas."

"It does, but I..." She sighed. "I just like art. I don't know all that much about it, really, but I like beautiful things."

"Remind me to show you my African

wood carvings someday,'' he said. He leaned back in the comfortable semicircular padded chair and lit a cigarette. ''Or don't you like art that exotic?''

''I have several African pieces of my own,'' she told him. ''Although I'm sure mine aren't as expensive as yours.''

''Stop that,'' he said coldly. ''I don't care for snobbery, inverted or not.''

She bit back a retort, busying herself instead with her coffee. The lunch had been perfect, and she shouldn't have attacked him. A twinge of color dotted her cheeks, and she let herself relax.

''I'm sorry,'' she said quietly.

The waiter came back before he could reply and while he was ordering strawberry shortcake for them, she studied him absently. He was, she thought, a striking man. Not exactly handsome. His brow was too jutting, his face too leonine, his jaw too square. It was a strong face, not a pretty one. His build was equally strong—husky as a wrestler, and narrow-hipped with powerful legs. He wasn't overly tall, but he didn't need to be. There was such raw power in his big body that he was as intimidating as any man two heads taller would have been. He really was quite attractive. Darkly, sensuously attractive. Her eyes rested briefly on the wide, chiseled perfection of his mouth, and she allowed herself to wonder, just for one mad instant, how it would feel to kiss him....

"Are you trying to memorize me?" Hawke asked quietly, as he caught her staring at him.

She blushed red as a cherry. "Sorry. I wasn't really looking at you," she lied glibly. "I was thinking about an assignment...."

"Was that it?" he asked, unconvinced. He caught her restless eyes and held them with an intensity that made her heart race. He'd never looked at her like that—not with that fiery, expressionless look that burned in his eyes. He held her gaze for so long, and with such raw power, that she was visibly shaken when she managed to drag her eyes down towards her coffee cup. She lifted it unsteadily to her lips.

"I...I don't really need dessert," she said softly.

"Yes, you do." He took a long draw from the cigarette. "What did Holland say about the trip? Has he convinced you that I'm going to ravish you the first night?"

She felt the color pour into her face. "Actually," she said huskily, "he thought you were a little too old to think of me in that respect."

"Well, I'll be damned," he said. "How old does he think I am, for God's sake, sixty?"

"Close," she remarked, avoiding his piercing eyes.

"How old do you think I am?" he asked suddenly.

She shrugged. "I've never thought about it."

"Liar." He took a swallow of his coffee and suddenly reached out to catch her cold, nervous hand in his, forcing her to look up into those threatening eyes.

"I'm seventeen years older than you, sparrow," he said in a deep, quiet tone. "But if I wanted you, those seventeen years wouldn't make a damned bit of difference to me. Or to you."

She felt her heart beating her to death from the inside. He'd never spoken to her like this, and it was devastating. Frightened, she drew her hand away from his and leaned back.

"What the hell difference does it make to Holland's mother if you go to Panama City with me?" he asked suddenly, harshly. "Are you engaged?"

She shifted uncomfortably. "He's asked me."

"And?"

"I don't want marriage," she replied. "Not now, not ever."

"Why?"

"Don't cross-examine me, Hawke, I'm not on the stand!" she cried.

"God, you're a puzzle," he remarked. He leaned one big arm over the back of his chair. He was wearing a light jacket over a pale blue shirt. The fabric stretched over the massive muscles of his chest. Under it, she could see the shadow of a mass of black, curling hair. Why did he have to be so masculine, so...

"I have to go..." she began weakly.

"Not yet," he said, gesturing toward the approaching waiter. "Not until I get a little more flesh on those bird bones."

"I'm not skinny!" she hissed at him as the waiter was walking away.

He dug into the massive dish of fresh strawberries and cream on their cake base, lifting an eyebrow as his eyes went pointedly to the soft rise and fall of her rounded breasts under the thin white blouse.

"Parts of you aren't," he corrected.

"Don't!" she whispered, attempting to give her entire concentration to the dessert.

"Doesn't Holland ever touch you, little one?" he asked gently.

She moved her thin shoulders as if trying to twist out from under the question. "Mark's a gentleman."

"Mark's a boy, Siri," he corrected.

"He suits me very well," she countered, savoring the sweet taste of the whipped cream. Her tongue came out to whisk it off her upper lip, and Hawke's eyes narrowed on the tiny movement. The deliberate scrutiny confused her, and she put the coffee cup quickly to her lips.

"Should I bring the camera?" she asked, trying to sound cool and professional.

"Only if you're planning to do a speculation piece on the 'Miracle Strip' for some travel magazine," he replied, "or photos for your album."

"Maybe," she said thoughtfully, "I could hire one of the hotel employees to pour beet juice over your head while I take pictures."

"I wouldn't advise it, honey," he said, mildly amused. "You might not like the way I'd reciprocate."

"You wouldn't hit that hard." She smiled.

His eyes travelled over her face, from the crown of golden hair to the amber eyes, the soft curve of her mouth. His gaze lingered there until her lips parted under the scrutiny that was as potent as a caress.

"Siri," he said in a deep, sensual tone, "if I ever lift my hand to you, it won't be to hit you."

The look in his eyes said much more than the words. It haunted her all the way back to the office.

Three

That lunch marked a turning point for Siri. Suddenly, the thought of Panama City, of being with Hawke for the better part of a week, was unbearable. And she knew when she reached her office that she wasn't going to go. No matter what, even if Bill fired her, she wasn't going. She took a deep breath and walked into his office.

"You're *what?*" Daeton exploded.

She stood her ground. "I'm not going with Hawke."

"Why, for God's sake?"

Now there, she thought miserably, was a good question. What could she tell him? I'm afraid of Hawke because of a look he gave me across a table?

She swallowed. "My...boyfriend doesn't like the idea," she said finally, digging up the only excuse he might find acceptable.

He threw down his pencil and leaned back in his chair. "Siri, there just isn't anybody else I can send," he explained. "Nobody. And even if there was, Hawke told your father that it was you or no one. This is one hell of a hot story. I don't want to blow it because your boyfriend's got a bad case of jealousy."

She stared at the cluttered top of his desk. "I'm sorry," she muttered, turning to open the door.

"Siri, if you do this to me," Bill Daeton threatened quietly, "I'll take you off the police beat and switch you to the garden club circuit for the next ten years.''

She shrugged fatalistically. ''I like flowers,'' she said over her shoulder, and closed the door.

If Daeton was disbelieving, her father was dumbstruck. He gaped at her over the dinner table, his face blank.

''Do you realize,'' he said quietly, ''how long it took me to convince Hawke to let you go?''

She smiled. ''Five minutes?'' she guessed.

''Four.'' He shook his head, toying with the brussel sprouts. ''Want to tell me why you changed your mind?'' he pursued.

''I'll sound silly.''

''Oh, I'm already convinced of that. Tell me anyway.''

She wrapped her cold fingers around her coffee cup. ''It's kind of hard to put into words,'' she began.

Jared spread his fingers behind his

head and leaned back lazily. "I've got all night."

"I thought you were taking Nadine to that new night club."

"Don't change the subject."

She shrugged. Of all people, she couldn't lie to her father. "I'm afraid of Hawke," she said miserably.

He didn't seem in the least surprised. "You've spent the past five years being alternately fascinated and terrified by him. Did you realize that you start backing away the minute he comes near you?" he asked with a patient smile.

She took the napkin from her lap and folded it. "Isn't this where I get the lecture about the evils of running away?" she asked.

"Just about." He leaned forward on his elbows. "He took you to lunch, didn't he?"

She nodded, dazed.

"Well, did he try to seduce you at the table?" he persisted.

"Of course not!"

"You needn't sound so indignant. I know Hawke," he laughed. "He isn't even vaguely subtle when he wants something, and that includes women."

"I didn't know he was such a playboy," she observed, wrapping both cold hands around her coffee cup.

"He isn't." He picked at a speck of lint on the sleeve of his jacket. "Oh, he's got money. But that can be a two-edged sword, my girl, didn't you know? I don't think he's ever been really sure if women want him or what he can give them."

"It wouldn't make a bit of difference if he didn't have a dime," she said without thinking.

Jared's grin went from ear to ear. "I didn't know you thought he was so attractive," he remarked, noting the sudden color in her cheeks.

"Even if he is a generation ahead of me, I can notice him," she said defensively.

"Age isn't everything, you know."

"It is to him," she grumbled absently. "Any day now, I expect him to offer to buy me a balloon or an ice-cream cone. Even now, with an award of merit under my belt for investigative reporting, he's still giving me the 'helpless little Siri' looks."

"You could change his mind if you tried," her father said gently.

"Why in the world would I want to?" she asked, aghast. "My gosh, dad, he's almost twice my age, and you know we don't get along at all. We never have!"

"Do you get along all that well with Holland?" he probed. "Honestly?"

She glowered at him. "I can handle Mark."

"That's probably the only reason you let him hang around, too," he said flatly. "And someday you'll accidentally marry him if you don't open your eyes!"

"I don't want to marry anybody," she muttered.

"It can still happen. Go with Hawke, Siri," he said, more solemn than she'd ever seen him. "Face it. Will you do that, for me?"

He didn't make sense, but at the suggestion, she gave way to a twinge of panic. She stood up, shaking her head stubbornly. "I'm sorry. I love you very much," she said, "but not enough for that. The story can go hang. I'm fresh out of sacrificial urges."

"Siri...!"

But she was already halfway up the staircase, running for privacy.

She knew her father wouldn't be back until late, so she threw on a deep blue caftan and stretched out in the living room on the couch with a book and put on a stack of easy listening records. The book should have taken her mind off the problem of Panama City, but she opened it and couldn't get past the front page.

It was almost a relief when the doorbell rang an hour later. Expecting that her father had lost his keys again, she threw open the door with a smile and a quip on her mouth and froze when she saw who was standing there.

"Oh!" she murmured.

Hawke raised an eyebrow at her, his dark eyes taking in every inch of her body outlined under the clinging blue fabric. He was obviously on his way home from a date, still dressed in his dark evening clothes. He had on a white ruffled shirt that was anything but effeminate, making his complexion seem even darker. His hand was propped against the door facing, and ruby cuff links gleamed rich and red in the light.

"Yes, 'oh'," he said. His eyes narrowed. "What the hell do you mean, you're not going with me?"

She swallowed hard, hating her nerve for deserting her as she stepped back to let him in the house. "I...well...you know..."

"I don't know. That's why I'm here. I

ran into your father and Nadine downtown. Siri, so help me, sometimes I think you belong back in high school instead of in a newspaper office!'' he growled.

She stared at the carpet, unaware of the picture she made with her blond hair curling delicately around her flushed face, her long lashes hiding the expression in her amber eyes.

''It's kind of hard to explain,'' she mumbled.

''Then let's do it over a nightcap.'' He took her arm firmly and propelled her back into the living room, while she tried desperately not to let him see how much his touch affected her.

He poured two drinks at the bar, handing her a sherry while he fixed himself a scotch on the rocks.

''I like scotch, too,'' she protested, glaring down at the pale red liquid in her glass.

''I like you sober. You cry when you're drunk,'' he taunted.

"Only that once!" she defended herself.

"Once was enough. Or have you forgotten...?"

"I'm sure trying to, if you'll let me!" she flashed back, embarrassed at the memory of how she'd clung to him in the car that night she overdid it at the senior prom, and he had to rescue her because Jared had been out of town.

He smiled down at her, something he rarely did, but there was a boldness in the dark eyes as he gazed over the clinging caftan again.

"I like you in blue," he said.

"Thanks," she murmured. She sipped the sherry nervously.

"Now tell me why you don't want to go."

She shifted restlessly. "Hawke, you know how Mark feels..."

"All I know is what a damned possessive jackass he is," he said shortly, the smile disappearing at the mention of her boyfriend. "I don't like the way he treats you. I never have."

"You don't understand!" she protested.

"The hell I don't!" His eyes narrowed into a piercing glare. Hers fell before their onslaught, and she clutched the glass like a shield.

He studied her downcast face for a long time, pausing to light a cigarette and take a long draw from it. "Now tell me the real reason, Siri," he said firmly. "You're afraid of me, aren't you?"

She couldn't meet his eyes, but she wasn't going to lie about it. She drew a slow breath. "Yes," she admitted.

A smile tugged at the corner of his chiseled mouth. "Why?"

She shook her head. "I don't know."

He took a draw from the cigarette. "Don't you?" he asked.

She lifted her eyes only to the top button of his shirt, quickly dropping them again.

"Hell, I don't know whether to be flattered or insulted," he said. "My God, Siri, you're still wet behind the ears."

She clenched her teeth. "I didn't mean it that way!"

"What other way is there? And look at me, dammit!"

Her eyes jerked up. She flushed at the intent, totally adult look he was giving her.

"You…you said…in the restaurant…" she grasped for words.

"I said what?" he growled. "That those seventeen years didn't matter? What the hell did you think I was talking about? Siri, if I meant to seduce you, I wouldn't have to take you all the way to Panama City!"

There it was, out in the open, and she'd never felt quite so stupid. She closed her eyes. "I…I feel pretty dumb."

"You're just young, sparrow," he said, kindly. "I understand you very well. Come with me."

She nodded. "All right."

"Holland will get over it," he assured her. "Tell him we'll send a joint post-card."

"He won't like it," she said with a wistful smile.

"Why the hell does it matter?"

"Because he's my—"

"Your what?" he shot at her. "Your lover?"

She glared at him. "No!"

"That I can believe." His dark eyes traced the supple lines of her body, and a musing smile touched his mouth. "He hasn't left a mark on you."

"What do you do? Brand your women?" she fired back.

He considered that for a minute, studying her through a thin veil of gray smoke. "Honey, if I'd had you, everybody who came in contact with you would see it written all over you," he replied flatly.

"In dollar signs?" she said venomously.

He smiled involuntarily. "Is my money my only attraction, little girl?"

She sighed loudly. "You ought to know it isn't," she said reluctantly. "Women follow you around like puppies."

"Children like me, too, don't you?" he retaliated.

"Ooooh!" she groaned, stamping her foot on the soft pile of the carpet. "Hawke Grayson, you make me so mad!"

"And your eyes burn like fiery topaz," he told her. Something wild and untamable flamed in his eyes for just an instant as they held hers. "Holland isn't man enough to kindle any fires in you, little bird, much less put them out."

"He suits me just fine, thanks."

"He wasn't suiting you at that restaurant the other night, was he?" he asked with a confident smile, as he threw down the last swallow of his drink. "It sounded like a down-home brawl from where I was sitting.''

''You and the scarlet lady, that is,'' she returned with a defiant glance in his direction.

One heavy eyebrow went up. ''Scarlet lady?'' he probed. ''Gessie? She types my letters, little girl, and answers the phone.''

''Excuse me,'' she apologized. ''I didn't know she could do all that on her back.''

He burst out laughing. ''You little brat! What the hell business is it of yours if I keep a mistress?''

She didn't want to think about that. ''None at all. And Mark isn't any of yours, either,'' she said stubbornly.

''We'll have to have a long talk about that someday.''

''My love life…!'' she began.

''What love life?'' he countered pointedly. ''You'd faint if he started to make love to you.''

"Mark," she said harshly, "is a gentleman!"

"God help him," he said with feeling. "What do you think men are made of, you little blond mule, ice water and spirits?"

"All of them aren't like you," she countered, feeling strangely out of her depth.

"Oh, to be twenty again, and so wise." He sighed heavily. "I appreciate the sentiment, little one, but with the amoral and licentious life I lead, it's hard to remember the innocent days of my youth."

"I doubt you were ever innocent," she muttered darkly.

"I was until my fourteenth birthday," he said, and smiled amusedly at the flush that burned her cheeks.

"Why don't you go home?" she asked hotly.

"I might as well," he remarked, studying his empty glass and her angry face.

"If you were waiting up for your father, you'd better sleep light. He and Nadine were going strong at the disco when I left."

"You, at a disco?" she said insultingly.

"How good are you?" he challenged.

"I'm young," she countered, "remember? We youths adjust to new steps better than you old people."

"By God, I ought to take you over my knee," he threatened.

She backed away, grinning. "Remember your blood pressure," she cautioned. "We wouldn't want you to have a stroke or anything."

His eyes kindled with amusement. "You damned little cat," he said.

"Flattery will get you nowhere, Mr. Grayson. Anyway, it's way past my bedtime, and you interrupted me right in the middle of *The Three Bears*."

He returned his empty glass to the bar,

stubbed out his finished cigarette, and started toward the front door.

"Remind me to send you a copy of the unedited version," he told her with a wry smile.

"Dirty old man," she said, blissfully unaware that she was flirting with him, or that it was the first time she ever had.

"Little brat," he countered. He turned as he started out the door. "Better start packing, Siri. I'm planning to fly down to Panama City in the morning. I'll call you in time to get breakfast before we leave."

"Okay. Hawke?"

He turned. "Yes?"

She shrugged apologetically. "I'm sorry I acted my age."

"You haven't, yet." He tugged at a strand of her wispy blond hair. "I don't think you know how."

"How to what?" she asked curiously.

"Goodnight, honey." He went down

the steps two at a time without bothering to answer her.

The next morning, sitting beside Hawke in the big Cessna he co-owned with her father, she wondered why she'd been so terrified of this trip. The weather was sunny, the plane was comfortable, and Hawke was actually being pleasant for once and not his usual sarcastic self. In fact, she was enjoying every minute of the flight.

Her one regret was that Mark hadn't accepted her decision to make the trip. She'd finally had to hang up on him on her way to the airport, amid ultimatums that he'd never see her again if she went. And while Jared might understand his daughter's sudden change of mind, Bill Daeton was still scratching his gray head trying to figure out his police reporter's strange behavior.

Siri sighed pleasantly and closed her eyes. For the next week, she wasn't going to let herself look backwards. She was going to enjoy the sand and the sun and the surf, and do her job, trying not to get in Hawke's way.

She glanced at him, noticing the hard, dark face that never seemed to relax, the rigid lines of his chin and mouth. They hallmarked the uncompromising personality of the man. Womanlike, she wondered if there was any tenderness under that stony exterior. No more of that, my girl, she warned herself firmly. Hawke was safe only so long as she thought of him as a big brother, a friend. She had a feeling he'd be totally devastating in a romantic role, and she was wary enough not to want to find out. With such a man, there'd be no freedom at all. It wouldn't be the way it was with Mark—a relationship that was comfortable, that made no demands, that left her to live as she pleased. Oh, no, Hawke would make demands. He'd want a woman who could match his own fierce spirit, who'd be as much a part of him as his own soul. He wouldn't settle for any easygoing relationship. She didn't know how she knew that, but she was sure she was not mistaken.

They landed in Panama City, and Hawke reached up to lift her to the ground from the metal step. It seemed almost as if he deliberately let her slender body slide slowly against his before he finally eased her feet to the pavement. His dark eyes held hers disturbingly the whole time, reading the effect on her flushed face.

"There's a restaurant here," he said as he released her. "Do you want to stop for a cup of coffee or go straight to the hotel?"

She took a deep breath of the hot, sea-smelling air. "I'd kind of like to get to the beach," she admitted, trying to disguise the childlike eagerness to wet her feet in the surf.

He only chuckled, as if he could pick

the thoughts out of her mind. "All right. I'll get a cab."

It was her first time in Panama City, and her eyes digested the atmosphere of it as they made the short trip from the airport to the hotel. The "Miracle Strip" gave a sweeping impression of blinding white sand and scruffy palm trees, beautiful modern hotels, and, most of all, traffic. It was noisy with the impatient sound of horns and voices calling back and forth, drowning out the distant sound of waves breaking against the beach. The predominant smell at the moment was not tangy sea air, but exhaust fumes from the tangle of automobiles.

"Disappointed?" Hawke asked beside her.

She flicked a glance at him, quick enough not to be caught by those wise, dark eyes. "A little," she admitted. "It's going to be terribly crowded."

"You're a reporter, remember?" he

taunted. "Crowds, and the people that compose them, are supposed to be your stock-in-trade."

"I get sick of people sometimes," she said absently, her eyes on the colorful, skimpy dress of tourists pouring from the motels on the wide highway. "I have to deal with them all day long, every day. Even when I get home at night, the phone always rings, and very rarely because of an emergency," she laughed. "Once I had a lady call me about putting an ad in a rival paper—at 11:30 at night, yet."

"Where would you be without those people?" he asked with a trace of a smile.

"Sleeping peacefully at night like everybody else," she quickly responded. Her eyes went to a flaming red hibiscus blooming against the brick wall of a motel they were passing, and she smiled involuntarily. "I don't know how I got to be a reporter in the first place," she mused, almost talking to herself.

"Crowds terrify me. I rarely even go to parties because I wind up sitting tucked away behind a potted plant with a glass frozen to my hands." She glanced at him. "Do you mind crowds? I don't suppose you could, being surrounded by them all the time."

"It goes with the job, honey," he replied. "A lawyer gets used to it."

"But do you really like it?" she persisted, meeting his eyes at last.

He reached out a big hand and twisted a strand of her soft hair around his fingers. The touch made her pulse race. "I like what I do. The kind of life my father preferred would have been the death of me."

"He...he built ships, didn't he?" she asked.

He caressed the strand of hair absently. "He was in shipping, Siri, when he wasn't frequenting casinos or sailing on the Aegean with some new playmate. Mother ran the business."

She dropped her eyes to the steady rise and fall of his chest. "Is she still alive?"

His eyes shifted to the white shoreline in the distance. "Both my parents are dead," he said flatly, and in a tone that didn't encourage her to pursue the subject.

"I don't mean to pry," she said gently. "I'm so used to asking questions…I suppose I ask too many sometimes."

He drew a deep breath and lit a cigarette. His dark eyes glanced at her. "Two different worlds, Siri," he remarked quietly. "I'm used to keeping secrets, while you're conditioned to revealing them. I'm a solitary man, little girl. Privacy is sacred to me."

She shrugged. "I thought I'd apologized," she said in a small voice, turning her attention out the window. She felt vaguely like a scolded child.

"For God's sake, don't pout!" he shot at her.

She flinched at the tone. "I'm not," she managed.

There was a brief silence. She wanted to sink right through the floorboard. He was angry with her, and she couldn't understand why. But it was like being a little bruised. Tears misted in her eyes, and she couldn't understand that, either.

"Siri," he said gently.

She kept her eyes averted, not answering him. The lump in her throat hurt.

"Siri," he repeated, and his big hand went out to force her chin up so that he could see her face. "Oh, damn!" he breathed when he saw the unshed tears.

"Will you just leave me alone?" she fired at him, jerking away from his hand.

A deep, harsh sigh came from the other side of the cab. He moved, catching her by the nape of her neck to press her face against the lightweight fabric of his summer suit jacket. "Let it out," he said at her temple. His arm circled around her shoulders, bringing her closer. "Let it out, Siri."

She fought the flood of tears, but they spilled over silently, running hot down her cheeks, onto the pale blue fabric. Her small hands clenched on his massive chest, as she relaxed against him with a choking sigh.

He pulled out a handkerchief and mopped her red face. "You don't even cry like a normal woman," he said softly.

"I never cry," she whispered, embarrassed, drawing away from him. "It wasn't allowed when I was growing up."

He brushed the damp hair away form her cheek. "Why?"

She shook her head. "Mother hated the sound of it. That's all I remember about her. I remember how she punished me for crying."

"What brought this particular cloudburst on?" he asked softly. His eyes narrowed dangerously. "Did you speak to Holland before we left?"

"Yes."

"What did he say?"

She lifted her face proudly. "That's my business, Hawke."

He reached out and touched her soft mouth with a dark, gentle finger, tracing its full outline. "I didn't mean to snap at you. There was a woman once, Siri. She used to blow up and pout if I looked at her sideways. You brought back a memory that sets fire to my temper."

"I didn't think a woman lived who would get that close to you," she remarked, as she mopped away the last traces of tears with the once-white handkerchief now stained with lipstick and mascara.

A mocking smile touched his hard mouth. "There was one until I found out she liked my money more than she liked me. The curse of being rich is that you never know whether people prefer the man or the wallet."

"Cynic," she accused. She shifted on

the seat to hand the handkerchief back to him. "If the money bothers you that much, why not donate it to charity?"

"To what charity?"

She grinned at him. "The Lonely Hearts society?" she suggested.

He chuckled softly at her impudence. "I'm not that lonely."

"Of course not. You probably have to lift the mattress every night to chase out the women," she agreed.

"What makes you think I keep women, you little innocent?" he challenged.

She studied the big masculine form beside her, the darkness of his face, the sensuality of his chiseled mouth, the massive chest that strained against the open shirt, where a nest of hair was just visible....

"Don't you?" she replied.

He caught her eyes and held them, just as he had that day in the restaurant, and something in the look made her blush.

He leaned forward, allowing the hand

holding his cigarette to rest against the
back of the seat while he caught her
cheek with the other hand, turning her
face toward him. His thumb passed
gently over her lips, parting them, pressing harder now, caressing the pearly
hardness of her teeth. She tasted the faint
tartness of tobacco on that tough skin,
and felt her pulse whipping her at the
touch that was openly seductive. His eyes
dropped to the inviting young softness of
her mouth.

Before either of them could move, or
speak, the cab pulled up in front of the
hotel and stopped. The moment of intimacy shattered into a thousand shimmer-
ing pieces, and was lost amid the subse-
quent routine of gathering possessions
and getting settled into new lodgings.

Hawke's secretary had booked them a
suite with bedrooms leading off opposite
sides of a huge sitting room. It was prac-
tical, but knowing Gessie's diabolical

train of thought, Siri took offense at the insinuation of it. Gessie knew that Hawke wouldn't think of taking advantage of his partner's daughter. But she also knew how compromising the arrangement would look to all concerned, especially to Mark Holland. Siri flushed with anger as she studied the suite.

Four

"**D**on't be such a damned little prude!" Hawke groaned irritably, reading the expression on her face. "I imagine your door has a lock, if you're that unnerved about sharing a suite with me."

"I didn't say a word," she countered, following him into the plush bedroom with its double bed where he set her case on the floor.

"You were thinking it," he said flatly. He studied her through narrowed eyelids.

"I was thinking what a trouble-making busybody your secretary is," she threw at him, eyes blazing. "How is this going to look if Mark finds out—and I'll bet you she'll find a way to make sure he's told!"

"I don't give a damn what he thinks," he said calmly.

"I do!"

He drew a deep, angry breath. "I came down here to work, Siri, not to have a running battle with you. Get your bathing suit on and we'll go down to the beach. Maybe the cold water will douse some of that hot temper before it triggers mine," he added roughly.

She shook back her hair. "I'm not trying to start an argument," she said apologetically. "Please, let's not quarrel."

"Why? Are you admitting that you're outgunned?" he asked.

Her eyes blazed. "Never!"

A wisp of a smile touched his hard

mouth. "I play to win, Siri," he said as he went out the door.

"If it's going to be war, you'll have to fly me to Fort Sumter," she called after him.

"So you can fire off the cannon?" he replied. He chuckled softly. "I think I'll take you to Charleston one day, and let you see the size of those old cannons."

"Gessie wouldn't like that," she said cattily.

He looked back at her from the doorway. "Push a little harder," he invited softly, "and I'll put you on the first charter flight leaving for Atlanta."

She glared at him. "We just got here!"

"Then behave, if you want to stay," he threatened, his eyes glittering.

She dropped her eyes to the carpet. "I'm not a child," she muttered.

"That," he replied heavily, "is the problem. Get your bathing suit on." And he left her standing there as he closed the door firmly.

* * *

It was her first bikini, although not her first two-piece bathing suit. But the thought of Hawke seeing her in the wispy, aqua bits of string-tied fabric made her uneasy. It would have been different with Mark, she thought, as she gathered her towel and started into the sitting room. Mark had a habit of never noticing what she wore. But Hawke's dark eyes spoke volumes when he saw her in anything particularly feminine. She wondered for an instant why she'd packed the bikini in the first place. It had been a last-minute whim, one that she regretted as she opened the door and walked into the sitting room.

Hawke was wearing a green, and blue patterned shirt unbuttoned over his bronzed chest, with a pair of white swimming trunks that left his powerful thighs bare. He had a towel over one shoulder and a lit cigarette in his hand. When he heard her door open, he turned from the window, his eyes openly interested, quiet, speculative as they traced deliberately every soft line and curve of her body in a silence that literally smouldered.

"God!" he breathed.

She blushed, feeling vaguely undressed by the look he was giving her. "I...I'm not used to this much bare skin," she murmured, trying to keep her own eyes off that hard, husky body with its taut brown skin and its covering of black, curling hair.

"That makes two of us," he said tightly. "Have you got a beach jacket?" he added harshly.

"Yes, but..."

"Then go get the damned thing and put it on!" he growled, turning back to the window.

"Yes, *sir!*" she breathed venomously. She went back into her room and shouldered into a thigh-length white terry cloth jacket, buttoning it up to her chin. She marched back into the sitting room with a towel held in a strangling grip.

"I'm ready when you are," she called over her shoulder, opening the door to march down the corridor, not caring whether or not he was following.

It was like being five again and having her father sling orders at her, she thought, feeling quite embarrassed. She found one bare spot on the beach, ignoring the blistering heat of the sand on her tender feet, and spread her big beach towel a few yards from the noisy surf. She slammed herself down onto it on her belly, pulling her dark glasses down to cover the hurt in her eyes. She didn't notice the children playing around her, building sandcastles and hunting sand crabs, or the couples wandering up and down in the surf. She felt crushed inside.

A movement beside her attracted her attention. Hawke spread down his own towel and lazily stretched out on his back, sunglasses hiding the expression in his eyes.

"Are you through having a tantrum?" he asked.

"Not quite," she replied tightly, pushing up on an elbow and facing him.

"When you are, you might consider taking off that jacket so the sun can get to you," he observed.

"You were the one who insisted I put it on," she reminded him sweetly.

He rolled over on his side, and she felt his eyes burning her. His hand went out to the top button of her beach jacket, undoing it with a deftness and sensuality that made her pulse race. Her breath was coming in quick and unsteady bursts.

"Do you have any idea," he asked softly, undoing the second button, "what it does to a man to look at a sweet young body and know that it's never been touched before?"

She felt the blush run the length of her as he finished the last button and leaned over to ease it off her shoulder. His fingers lingered for a moment on the creamy skin at her collarbone.

"I'm not immune to you, little virgin," he said in a deep, soft tone. "I may be over the hill in your young eyes, but my instincts are in excellent condition, and I still respond like a healthy male. Don't trust those seventeen years to keep you chaste, Siri. I can lose my head just like any other man. Especially," he added quietly, "when you encourage me to lose it."

"I don't know what you mean!" she whispered unsteadily.

"Yes, you do." He rolled over onto his back. "You put that bikini on deliberately, sparrow."

She closed her eyes and lay back down on her stomach. She wanted to deny it, but he'd have seen through the lie, and she knew it.

"It's perfectly normal, Siri," he murmured lazily. "You're young enough to want to test your ability to attract men. Just don't test it on me.''

''I'm sorry,'' she said in a strangled tone. ''I think I must be going crazy.''

''You're only growing up, little girl,'' he replied, ''and it's about time. Stop brooding about it.''

''I'm not brooding, I'm embarrassed,'' she admitted tightly.

He reached out and caught her hand where it lay on the towel, pressing it gently. ''Nothing you could do would embarrass me. But if you try to seduce me, I'll put you over my knee. I think too much of Jared to play fast and loose with his daughter.''

''You aren't mad at me?'' she asked hesitantly.

He smiled. ''No, honey.'' He let go of her hand, shifting as two little boys leapt over his legs. ''Watch out,'' he warned her with a chuckle.

She dodged the little feet just in time.

"I was afraid somebody was going to walk on me," she murmured.

"It's human nature," he remarked.

"What is?"

"The urge to step on people when they lie down and ask for it," he replied, amusement in his deep voice.

"You'll probably never feel it," she remarked, studying the size and powerful masculinity of his husky form. His legs were broad and powerful. He had a natural bronze tan that had nothing to do with sunlight. Muscular, masculine, he drew a woman's eyes like a magnet. He was vividly exciting in swimming trunks, especially compared with the skinny white bodies of most of the other men on the beach.

"You're staring, baby," he said suddenly, and she turned her face away with a flush of embarrassment.

"I was thinking," she corrected hotly.

"You must think a hell of a lot these days," came the bland reply.

She shifted restlessly on her towel. "Where do we start looking for your witness?" she asked, attempting to change the subject.

"In the hotel bar," he replied lazily. "I hope you've got your driver's license with you. Right now you look about sixteen."

"Is that a compliment or an insult?" she muttered.

"A little bit of both, sparrow." He stretched his big arms above his head and sighed. "God, I needed this! I can't remember a rougher week."

"I know what you mean," she replied. "Remember that controversy about the ambulance service not answering a call, when that teenager almost bled to death? Bill sent me to get the story."

"Did they fry you?" he asked.

"With onions," she sighed. "I felt two inches high when I walked out. It wasn't one of the regular ambulance service technicians who answered the call and refused to make it; it was a cocky young rookie who only signed on for a few weeks during a break in his schedule. He was fired the day after the incident. But nobody told us that." She again sighed wearily. "I hate this stinking business sometimes. Those men care, Hawke. Most of them really care, and they don't make fortunes, either. They do a thankless job and the only publicity they ever get is when something like this happens. They get crucified for their mistakes, by well-meaning people like me."

"If you didn't do it, who would?" he asked quietly, slanting a glance in her direction. "The taxpayers are entitled to know how their funds are being spent or misspent. That's what your job is all about, Siri, observing and reporting, not judging. And for objectivity, on a scale of ten, I'd give you a nine plus."

That made her smile. "Thanks. But I still feel like a 14K creep." She sat up on the towel, folding her arms around her raised knees, leaning her chin on them. "Hawke, who are we looking for?"

"No notebook?" he commented drily. He then watched her dig in her beach bag and produce a small pad and a pen.

"Okay, shoot," she said smugly.

He smiled as he lit a cigarette and blew out a cloud of smoke. "Do you carry it into the tub?" he asked.

"Sure!"

He raised an eyebrow. "As to who we're looking for, remember when the landlady was rousted out of bed at three in the morning to open the door to Devolg's room for that 'concerned friend'?"

"The one who mysteriously disappeared when the landlady got the door open and found Devolg, lying on his bed stabbed to death?" she replied.

"The same."

"Hawke, is that who we're looking for?" she asked excitedly.

"Let's just say I've got a hunch who

the man was, and I've a contact here who may be able to unravel the mystery for me," he said solemnly. He took another draw from his cigarette. "If I'm right," he mused with a dark smile, "it's going to blow one big hole in the prosecution's case."

"You think the boy is innocent?" she asked.

"My God, Siri, would I have taken the case if I thought he wasn't?" he asked harshly.

"I never try to second-guess you," she replied. "It's not worth the wear and tear on my nerves. Are you going to give me a name?"

"What do you think, honey?" he asked nonchalantly.

"I think hell will freeze over first."

"Shrewd perception."

"If you're not going to tell me anything, why did you agree to let me come along?" she asked, peering at him over the top of her pad.

His head turned toward her, but she couldn't see his eyes through the dark lenses of his sunglasses. He didn't say a word, but she felt vaguely uneasy.

"Hawke, what will you do if the prosecution gets to your mystery man first?"

Both dark eyebrows went up. "What do you think they'd do, bump him off? Honest to God, Jared needs to take those detective novels away from you."

She shrugged. "James Bond..." she began.

"...is a remarkable piece of fiction, but fiction, nevertheless. Why," he asked himself, "*did* I bring you along?"

"Because you promised Dad." A mischievous smile touched her pink bow of a mouth. "Hawke, can I play in the sand now? Will you buy me a bucket and a shovel?"

His chiseled lips made a thin line as his head turned once again in her direction. "Aren't you a little old for these kind of games?" he asked shortly.

She felt whipped. "Can't I even tease you, for Pete's sake?" she asked irritably.

"Not that kind of teasing, no!" he growled.

"You're as touchy as a sunburned water moccasin," she grumbled.

"I thought you came out here to sunbathe," he remarked.

She stretched out on her towel with an irritated sigh. "So I did," she murmured, but she was talking to herself.

Supper in the hotel restaurant was the best she'd ever had, perhaps because her swim in the Gulf had whetted her appetite, or maybe because Hawke was in a better mood. He seemed more relaxed, as if the delicious meal had taken the edge off the black humor he'd been in most of the day.

She liked the way he looked in his cinnamon colored silk shirt, worn with a lightweight beige suit that made him stand out from the crowd. He was, she thought miserably, such a handsome man; not in the conventional sense, but in a rugged, very masculine way that made her fingers want to reach out and touch him. It was a feeling she'd never experienced before. It puzzled and frightened her, all at once.

She concentrated on her coffee. "When do we go to the bar?" she asked.

"In," he studied the watch strapped in the curling dark hair on his wrist, "ten minutes. I contacted my informant by phone." His dark eyes met hers across the table. "You'll have to pretend to be invisible, sparrow. I don't want anyone in that bar, especially the man I'm meeting there, to believe you're anything other than my date. It's a dangerous game, hunting a murderer. In that respect, your precious mystery writers have a valid point."

"But, Hawke…" she protested.

"My terms, Siri," he reminded her.

"And you agreed to them. I want you kept out of this as much as possible. I'll tell you what I want you to know, when the time is right."

"Male chauvinist," she grumbled. "I can take care of myself."

"I'm going to let you prove that one of these days. But for now, you'll do what I tell you," he said darkly.

"Yes, Uncle Hawke," she said in her best juvenile voice. "Will you buy me an ice-cream soda?"

His eyes narrowed. "Keep digging me, and you'll wish to God I *was* your uncle."

She made a face at him. "Honestly, you and my father…!"

"Do you think I want to find your body washed up on some godforsaken stretch of beach because you flirted with danger one time too many?" he demanded hotly. "I'd give blood if Bill Daeton would take you off that police beat. You like the risk just a little too much for my peace of mind.''

''You're not my keeper!'' she flung at him.

His eyes narrowed, sliding boldly over the bodice of her beige dress, and it was almost as if he was touching her.

''Do you burn like that with a man, Siri?'' he asked in a soft, low voice. ''Has Holland ever tapped those deep fires?''

She felt herself flushing. ''I'd like to go now.''

''Afraid to talk about it with me?'' he taunted.

''The lobster was delicious,'' she replied as she rose.

He chuckled softly, walking behind her to the cashier. There was something almost predatory in the sound of his soft laughter.

She didn't believe for a minute that she might wind up being washed in on a wave with her throat cut, but Hawke was

so doggedly protective of her that it made
her uneasy. He seated her in a booth in
the darkened bar where the jukebox
blared like an orchestra in a closet, deaf-
ening and brassy. He ordered her a
sherry, ignoring the dirty look she gave
him.

"Stay put," he said, leaning over to
growl in her ear so that he could make
her hear him over the music. "I'll be at
the bar."

"Hawke, why are you being so..."

He caught her soft throat with one big
hand and pressed her head back against
the cold leather of the booth, his mouth
hovering just above hers. He held her
eyes for a long, static moment. His hand
moved, testing the effect of the look with
a finger at the stampeding pulse in her
throat.

The noise, laughter and flickering can-
dlelight faded away and there was only
Hawke, bending over her, with his eyes
appearing almost black under those

darkly knit brows as he studied her. His
fingers lifted to her mouth, touching her
lips, whispering across them, making
them part as her breath whispered fran-
tically past them.

His thumb gently pressed down on her
lower lip as he bent. Dazed, her eyes
dwelt on the chiseled perfection of his
mouth as it opened slightly just before he
leisurely fitted it to hers. It was a tantalizing kiss, so brief and light and teasing
that it felt more like a fleeting breeze. But
the effect it had on her was evident in her
trembling pulse, the breathless sigh that
passed her lips, the slender young hand
that involuntarily lifted in protest when
he drew away.

His forefinger pressed against her
mouth for an instant, and he smiled at her
with a quiet, tender warmth that made
lightning spark in her mind.

Siri gazed after him, helplessly. Of
course, he'd planned it, it was part of the
charade. But his mouth had been hard,

and tasted of tobacco and mint, and she ached for something more violent than that whisper of promise. What would it be like, she wondered dazedly, to let him kiss her the way he must kiss Gessie; to feel the hunger and rough passion in that eager mouth, to let him touch her....

She jerked her mind back into place as the waitress brought the mild drink he'd ordered for her. She took a long, deep swallow of it and willed her strung nerves to relax. She couldn't afford to think about him like that. Hawke wasn't a manageable boy like Mark. He was a man, and he didn't play games. The chaste kisses she was used to wouldn't come near to satisfying someone like Hawke; she knew that without being told. And, for her, anything deeper was out of the question. She couldn't make that kind of commitment.

Her eyes involuntarily sought him out. He was talking to someone now; a tall, skinny blond man with a mustache. Their

conversation was intent, and Hawke frequently nodded. The blond man finished
his drink and left the bar. Hawke came
back to the booth, carrying a tumbler of
what was obviously scotch and water on
the rocks.

"Well?" she asked loudly, hoping that
her nervousness wouldn't show.

He finished the drink in one swallow.
"We've got to talk. Let's go upstairs."

She gathered up her purse and followed him, away from the shuddering
impact of the music. She didn't want to
go back to that lonely suite with him. Not
yet, not feeling this kind of longing when
he could read her expressions like the
weather report. But, there was no hope
for it. And she was curious about what
had happened to make him look so solemn.

Going down the hall, Siri sidestepped
to keep from colliding with another couple and heard Hawke's sudden, deep,
"Well, I'll be damned!"

"That depends on how good you are between now and the day your number's up," came the laughing reply from the tall, blond man who grabbed Hawke's outstretched hand and shook it heartily. "Hawke Grayson! God, it's been years! The only time I see you now is on the news or in the papers. You remember Kitty, don't you?"

Hawke grinned down at the petite little blonde hanging on to the tall man's sleeve. "How could I ever forget your wife?" he asked. "Just as pretty as ever, too."

"You lawyers are all alike," Kitty said through a blush, smiling shyly at the husky, dark man.

"Randy, Kitty, this is my partner's daughter, Cyrene Jamesson," Hawke said, introducing the couple to his puzzled companion. "Siri, these are the Hallers. Randy and I went through law school together. Our families were neighbors in Charleston."

"I'm very glad to meet you," Siri said politely.

"Ah, that's because you don't know us yet," Randy told her with a twinkling smile.

"Honestly, Randy," Kitty muttered. "Siri, you'll have to excuse him, it's spending so much time around crazy people that does this to him."

Siri grinned back. "I know all about crazy people."

"Amen," Hawke said with a long-suffering expression. "Meet the poor man's Lois Lane. Siri," he explained, "is a police reporter."

"So you report policemen." Randy smiled blankly. "Good for you. Who do you report them to?"

"It runs in his family, you know," Kitty said in a conspiratorial tone. "His grandfather was a ballet dancer."

"My God, why did you have to shame me like that?" Randy groaned. "Conjuring up images of an old man parading in a pink ruffled tutu.''

"How would you like to come up to our suite for coffee?'' Kitty asked quickly. "If you're not in a hurry....''

Hawke took Siri's arm. "No hurry,'' he replied. "We'd enjoy it.''

"Of course,'' Siri seconded, but her mind was on what Hawke had discovered in the bar.

Siri liked the Hallers. Randy possessed not only a keen wit, but an inquiring mind to go with it; a fact that became quickly apparent the minute he and Hawke began discussing law. Kitty was open and friendly and simply loveable. She and Siri found an instant rapport and spent the rest of the evening comparing notes on art, music and books, leaping from one subject to the next, fired by the rapid exchange of viewpoints.

"Ladies, I hate to break this up,'' Hawke said finally, "but it's past this youngster's bedtime." Ignoring her outraged look, he reached down and pulled her up from the sofa with a firm hand.

"Yes, Uncle Hawke," she muttered with a false pout, and Randy's laughter burst the silence.

"That's a new role for you, Hawke," Randy observed.

"Yes, it is," came the deep, drawled reply, while the hard glance that went Siri's way along with it promised early retribution. "Come on, Miss Pain-in-the-neck, we've got a long day ahead of us tomorrow."

"Not all of it, I hope," Kitty said. "We're going to that marine world place down the road, and we were going to invite the two of you along."

Hawke glanced down at Siri. "Want to?" he asked.

She smiled at Kitty. "I've never been to one before."

"We'll leave here about ten in the

morning,'' Randy said with a grin, ''if that's not too early.''

''Not at all,'' Hawke replied. ''And before you start getting ideas, Siri and I are working on a case, not each other. She's spoken for,'' he added.

Randy seemed to flush, but he recovered quickly. ''I have to admit, I wondered, even though she is a little younger than your normal… That is… Oh, hell, we'll see you in the morning.''

Hawke nodded with a wispy smile. ''Goodnight.'' He drew Siri along with him, leaving her to call her goodbyes over her shoulder.

He unlocked the door to their suite and let her in, locking it firmly behind him as he faced her with angry dark eyes.

Five

"Now," he began in a low, quiet tone, "what's this 'Uncle Hawke' business."

"Why did you have to make such an issue out of it being strictly business in front of the Hallers?" she countered, still feeling the embarrassment. "I'm sure they weren't thinking anything of the sort! Look at the age difference!"

His eyes went slowly up and down her body. "I'm looking," he replied quietly.

"And I'll remind you that it didn't seem to matter to you in the bar. You wanted more."

She felt herself turning red. Her lips parted, but she couldn't make a sound. She turned away, folding her arms across her slender body, feeling again the hunger, the newness of passion.

"Remind me at some appropriate time," he said shortly, "to give you a brief lecture on the danger of provocation."

She felt her heart pounding under her ribs. "I...wasn't trying to provoke you."

"Smart girl," he replied. She felt his eyes on her. "Just keep in mind that I'm past the age of hand holding and chaste kisses. If I ever start making love to you, I won't stop."

She felt the color burning in her cheeks, and she whirled to face him with her eyes widening in something between disbelief and outrage. "I...I wouldn't let you!"

"Yes, you would; because I'd know how to make you." He paused to light a cigarette, but his eyes never left hers. "You react to me in a way that makes my blood splinter, little girl. You may think it's carefully hidden, but I don't miss much." His eyes darkened. "I could rouse you to a kind of passion you never dreamed existed, and in minutes I could make you give me what you've never given any man."

"You couldn't!" she whispered huskily.

One dark eyebrow went up with a corner of his mouth. "Would you like me to prove it, Siri?" he asked gently.

Her eyes widened. Just the thought of it made her tremble. She knew he could, it was written all over her. But it wouldn't mean anything to him, except a new conquest, and she knew that, too. With a sound resembling a sob, she turned away, opening the sliding glass doors to walk out onto the cool balcony.

In this distance, she could see the chain reaction of the waves as they hit the beach in a watery white rhythm, with a sound that was violent yet strangely soothing.

She heard his step behind her, and smelled the tang of cigarette smoke in the semi-darkness.

"Did I wound you, sparrow?" he asked calmly.

She rubbed her hands over the chill on her arms. "I'm not bleeding," she replied coolly. "I'm tough enough, Hawke. My line of work requires it as much as yours does."

There was a deep sigh behind her. "Randy's known me for a lot of years. This is the first time he's ever seen me with a woman in a hotel when it was innocent. I didn't want either of them thinking you were the kind of woman I usually carry around with me."

The statement made her turn to face

him, her eyes wide and curious. "But they'd probably never see me again…?"

He didn't say anything, but his eyes were intent on her face, and she saw his jaw clench as she looked up at him.

She dropped her eyes. "I'm sorry," she murmured. "I've been touchy this week. It's my fault. I…I don't know why."

"I do," he said softly. "But there isn't a damned thing I can do about it." Before she could pick up on that, he moved to the balcony railing. "Siri, I've got a good lead but it's going to mean leaving you here for a day or so while I run it down."

"Tomorrow?"

"The day after. Can you amuse yourself until I get back?"

"Of course. But can't I come along?" she asked.

She saw the white flash of teeth as he grinned. "If you want to share a bed with me. I'll be staying in a friend's apartment."

She knew without being told that the friend in question was female. She felt vaguely betrayed and angry.

"I didn't think it was ethical to get information that way," she said tightly.

"What way?" he asked imperturbably.

"Well, it's a woman, isn't it?" she asked.

"Yes."

"Then..."

"You'd better quit while you're ahead," he remarked with patient amusement. "I might get the impression that you're jealous."

"Me? Jealous? Of you? The idea!" she exclaimed.

He chuckled softly, dangerously. "If you were a few years older, or only a little more sophisticated, I'd take you to bed and teach you what being a woman is all about."

"You...you...how...!" she sputtered. Before she let her temper get the best of her at his merciless teasing, she ran back into the suite, into her bedroom, and locked the door loudly behind her. Of all the maddening men in the world, Hawke Grayson was definitely at the top of the list! In the distance, she heard again the soft, dangerous sound of his deep laughter.

The taunting left its mark on her. She was withdrawn the next morning as she and Hawke rode along the white satin coast with Randy and Kitty. She was thankful for Randy's chatter which made it unnecessary for her to carry on a conversation.

It seemed like no time at all before they got to the marine world complex, an enormous circular building with people streaming in and out. Even though it was crowded, Siri reacted to it with the same eager curiosity that had led her into reporting. Everything here was new, exciting, and she felt like a child in a candy store.

The dolphins in the aquarium outside were beautiful and sleek, looking so delicately gentle for all their size that she felt a sudden surge of compassion for them. It was sad that animals of such remarkable intelligence that they could save men in the sea, and communicate with each other in their own unique language, were reduced to the level of performing dogs.

"Aren't they beautiful?" Kitty sighed, smiling as the trainer held a fish over the tank, which the dolphin leapt up to take gently out of his hand.

"In the open sea, yes," Siri said vaguely. "Here, imprisoned..."

"It beats having them slaughtered by Japanese fishermen," Hawke remarked, watching her closely.

She nodded as she met his probing eyes, amazed at the way he had of reading her mind.

"She doesn't like zoos, either," Hawke told their two companions with a half smile. He caught Siri by the hand and pulled her along with him. "I'll take her downstairs to see the turtles."

"Do people eat sea turtles?" Siri asked as they went down the steps to the darker level of the building.

"Yes, honey, they do. But not these," he added. "God, you're a little crusader."

"I can't help it if I don't like to see things caged," she muttered.

He turned her to him by the wall, out of the way of other tourists, and looked down into her flushed face. "Including people?"

"Including people," she said reluctantly. "I...I don't like being a possession," she added uneasily.

His big hands moved caressingly to her shoulders. "How would you know, little girl," he asked in a deep, slow voice, "when you've never been possessed?"

She blushed, meeting the teasing look in his eyes. "You don't know that."

"Don't I, sparrow?" he asked softly. He drew her slowly against his broad, hard body, feeling her stiffen even at the light contact. The implied intimacy of the action, as she felt his broad thighs touch her own, caused her to draw back as if she'd been burned.

"Coward," he murmured. "What could I do to you here?"

She pulled gently away from him and concentrated on the shell exhibits all around the well-lit room. Inside, she was trembling with the newness of that note in Hawke's deep voice, from the unfamiliar fire in his eyes when he'd looked at her.

"Don't panic," he said at her shoulder, "I was only teasing, Siri."

"I...I'd like it if you wouldn't," she replied tightly. "You said yourself once that I was still wet behind the ears. I know I am, but it hurts to have you make fun of it."

His hands touched her waist lightly,

and she felt his breath in her hair. "God knows I'm not making fun of you, sparrow," he said quietly.

"Then why do you…"

"God, baby, what can I do?" he asked huskily.

"I don't understand."

But before she could turn around, or he could answer, Randy and Kitty joined them and the rest of the afternoon went by quickly as they discovered one tourist attraction after another. It was at the last one, the snake palace, that Siri balked.

"Oh, no," she said quickly, hanging back as the other three started toward the enclosed building with its gaudy pictures of vicious-looking reptiles. "I'd rather bleed to death than walk in there."

"Are you afraid of snakes?" Kitty asked gently.

"Oh, no," Siri denied, "I'm terrified of them!"

"You two go ahead," Hawke told them. "I'll keep Siri company."

"You don't have to do that," Siri protested quickly, and the snakes began to look better and better to her. "I can..."

"Hawke? Hawke!" came a sultry, surprised voice from behind them.

They turned, just in time to see a dark, petite little brunette throw herself into Hawke's arms and pull his head down to kiss him feverishly. Siri turned away from the sight, which went through her like a flaming lance.

"Oh, Hawke!" the brunette cooed softly, with more than a trace of Spanish accent, "what a wonderful surprise to find you here! Can you come back with Renaldo and me for a drink?"

"I'm with friends, Angel," he replied with a smile.

"No importa," Angel said breezily, "bring them, too! I've got a villa near here, with miles and miles of beach. And Renaldo would love to talk over old times with you."

"Where is your brother?" he asked,

puncturing Siri's vain hope that the missing "Renaldo" might be the woman's husband.

"Back there. Rey...Rey!" Angel called, and a strikingly tall, dark man came wandering up to join the small group. His eyes swept over Siri's slender body.

"You remember Hawke, don't you?" Angel asked with a flash of white teeth.

"Most assuredly," Rey said. "A pleasure. And this is...?" he asked, swinging without warning to face Siri, his eyes level and plainly interested.

"My partner's daughter, Siri Jamesson," Hawke replied with a curtness in his tone that was lost on Rey.

"A pleasure," the Latin repeated, and lifted Siri's hand to his lips.

Hawke introduced Randy and Kitty, and Angel persisted until she got her way and had them back in the rented car headed for her villa. Oh, well, Siri thought wearily, at least she had escaped the snakes.

But when they got to the hacienda-style villa with its seemingly acres of untouched beach, Siri wondered if the snakes just might not have been better. Between Angel's openly seductive manner toward Hawke and Rey's dead-tilt efforts to catch Siri's wary eye, it was like being caged with tigers.

The worst of it was the familiarity between Hawke and the little brunette. They were more than just old friends, and it showed. Why it should have mattered so much, Siri didn't know. But it mattered. She wanted to get out, to run, to go home. She couldn't bear the way his dark eyes played on Angel's face, and she didn't understand her own indignation.

"What do you do, Miss Jamesson?" Rey asked politely, perching himself comfortably on the arm of the massive chair she was sitting in. "Are you an attorney like your father?"

"I'm a reporter."

"A reporter!" His eyes brightened with interest.

Siri laughed. "I work for a daily newspaper, but I cover the police beat; fires, wrecks, murders, those kind of stories. And believe me, there's nothing funny about that."

"A woman involved in such tragic work?" he exclaimed. "You must have nerves of iron!"

"Not really," Siri admitted, sipping the rum punch in her tall glass. "What do you do?"

He shrugged. "Not much of anything," he admitted. He grinned. "I have, fortunately, the means to pursue a life of pleasure."

"How nice," she murmured appropriately.

"Yes, it is."

She glanced at him, mentally comparing him with Hawke, who also had the means to pursue a life of pleasure, but preferred useful work that also had its dangers. Hawke didn't seem to care for Angel's brother, and she wondered if he didn't remind him of his own father; a pleasure seeker, uninvolved and uncaring except for his own idle pursuits. It didn't sound like much of a life, but she kept quiet. To each his own, she thought.

"I wish I had not promised to join my friends for a cruise," Rey said. "I would much prefer to spend the time with you."

"Unfortunately," she smiled, "I have very little time to spend on pleasure. I'm a working girl, and I'm here on assignment. I have to account for my days."

"You are not...how you say... Hawke's woman?" he asked.

She glared at him. "I have a steady boyfriend back home who suits me very well," she said with ice in her tone. "I'm here working on a story, of which Hawke is part. That's all. Period. I am not available for fun and games for bored playboys!"

"Please, Siri, you misunderstand…!"
Rey began quickly, his face going rather
white at the tone of her voice.

"I don't think so," she told him, ris-
ing. She moved back to where Kitty was
sitting and squeezed in beside her, leaving the stunned Latin behind her.

Hawke glanced toward her, then toward the glass she was holding, and she
read the amusement in his dark eyes. It
made her flush uncomfortably. I'm not
tipsy, she wanted to yell at him. In defi-
ance, she lifted the glass to her lips again.

"Having trouble, honey?" Kitty whispered, squeezing her hand.

"Not any more," she replied smugly,
and finished the rum punch while the others sailed forth on the subject of ships.

Rey left soon afterwards with a really
wounded look about him. Siri half regretted what she'd said, but not that she'd
said it. She didn't have time to fight off
an amorous Latin in whom she wasn't really interested.

If she'd been hoping for an early departure, her hopes were doomed to disappointment. Angel insisted that the small group stay for a meal. She had her combination housekeeper-cook busy in the kitchen before anyone could protest.

Siri hated the ordeal of watching Angel smother Hawke. She hated even more the fact that he didn't seem to mind her attentions. It went from bad to worse when the little Spanish woman turned on her expensive stereo system and flooded the room with soft, seductive music. She threw back the carpet and invited the others to dance, pointedly ignoring the fact that Siri didn't have a partner as she glued herself to Hawke's broad body.

Randy, a gentleman from the shoes up, asked Siri to dance, but she quickly shook her head with a convincing smile.

"Oh, I don't dance," she said quickly, "but thanks all the same."

She dodged the incredulous look Hawke threw her over Angel's bare shoulder and curled up on the sofa with a magazine about the latest fashions. Did Angel have to dance that close to him, she wondered, darting a green glance their way. Did she have to press so close, and tangle her hands in that softly curling hair at the nape of his broad neck? Did she have to look so bloody content?

As soon as it was humanly possible, she promised herself that she was going to get out of that room and make herself scarce until supper. She'd never felt more suffocated. She had the oddest feeling that Angel found her threatening, and it puzzled her. There wasn't anything between her and Hawke, wasn't it obvious? After all, Siri sighed, remembering her nose that was too short, her eyes that were too big, her hair that was too silvery to be a true blonde—she was no competition for that spicy Latin. So why was Angel throwing her the icy looks?

While she was working that out, she failed to hear the phone ring, or see the

Play the

"LAS VEGAS" GAME

GET 3 FREE GIFTS!

FREE GIFTS!

FREE GIFTS!

FREE GIFTS!

FREE GIFTS!

TURN THE PAGE TO PLAY! Details inside!

Play the "LAS VEGAS" Game

and get

3 FREE GIFTS!

FREE GIFTS!

FREE GIFTS!

1. Pull back all 3 tabs on the card at right. Then check the claim chart to see what we have for you — 2 FREE BOOKS and a gift — ALL YOURS! ALL FREE!

2. Send back this card and you'll receive brand-new Silhouette Desire® novels. These books have a cover price of $4.75 each in the U.S. and $5.75 each in Canada, but they are yours to keep absolutely free.

3. There's no catch. You're under no obligation to buy anything. We charge nothing — ZERO — for your first shipment. And you don't have to make any minimum number of purchases — not even one!

4. The fact is, thousands of readers enjoy receiving their books by mail from the Silhouette Reader Service™. They enjoy the convenience of home delivery...they like getting the best new novels at discount prices, BEFORE they're available in stores...and they love their *Heart to Heart* newsletter featuring author news, horoscopes, recipes, book reviews and much more!

5. We hope that after receiving your free books you'll want to remain a subscriber. But the choice is yours — to continue or cancel, any time at all! So why not take us up on our invitation, with no risk of any kind. You'll be glad you did!

Visit us online at
www.eHarlequin.com

FREE!
No Obligation to Buy!
No Purchase Necessary!

Play the
"LAS VEGAS" Game

PEEL BACK HERE ▶
PEEL BACK HERE ▶
PEEL BACK HERE ▶

YES! I have pulled back the 3 tabs. Please send me all the free Silhouette Desire® books and the gift for which I qualify. I understand that I am under no obligation to purchase any books, as explained on the back and opposite page.

326 SDL DNX9   225 SDL DNYF

FIRST NAME	LAST NAME

ADDRESS

APT.#	CITY

STATE/PROV.	ZIP/POSTAL CODE

(S-DB-09/02)

7 7 7	GET 2 FREE BOOKS & A FREE MYSTERY GIFT!
♣ ♣ ♣	GET 2 FREE BOOKS!
🍒 🍒 🍒	GET 1 FREE BOOK!
🔔 🔔 🔔	TRY AGAIN!

DETACH AND MAIL TODAY

The Silhouette Reader Service™ — Here's how it works:

housekeeper motioning to Angel. She missed the sudden intent look in Hawke's dark eyes as he started toward her. She felt him catch her hand, and she gasped with surprise. She hadn't realized he was so close.

"Dance with me, sparrow," he said quietly.

She let him pull her to her feet and lead her out onto the bare wood floor. His big arms enveloped her close against his broad, husky body until air could barely have gotten between them. She felt the tremor go through her slender body and wondered at the strength and newness of what she was feeling.

The sun was just beginning to go down outside the huge picture window, darkening the room gently, intimately. The slow, sultry pace of the music made the atmosphere all that much more intimate, and Randy and his young wife were already oblivious to their surroundings as they danced a few feet away.

Drowning in new sensations, Siri moved close to Hawke. Obeying an instinct as old as time, her hands slid up over his broad chest to tangle gently in the thick hair that curled just slightly at the nape of his powerful neck.

"Siri..." he warned softly, something tight and odd in his tone as his big hands contracted bruisingly at her waist.

She nestled her head against his chest with a sigh, letting the music and the nearness wash over her as the amber glow of a setting sun added to the magic of being close against Hawke like this, making her feel reckless.

Her fingers caressed the back of his head slowly, gently. Against her slenderness, she could feel the heavy, driving beat of his heart through the thin fabric of his shirt. The blazing warmth of his chest caressed her cheek.

"Do you know what you're doing to me?" he asked gruffly, his grip tightening painfully.

"You didn't grumble when Angel did it," she murmured drowsily.

"Angel wouldn't mind the consequences. You would," he said flatly.

She moved closer. "Are you sure?" she whispered softly.

His big hands moved up to the back of her head, forcing her face up to his dark, blazing eyes. "You'd better be," he warned huskily.

Something in the way he was looking at her made her blood run wild through her veins. Her fingers reached up and touched his mouth gently, sensually. "Oh, Hawke..." she whispered, her eyes soft with faint pleading as they met his.

"Watch the table!" Kitty called, but it was too late. Siri hit it with her hip, and it was just bruising enough to break the spell.

She drew slightly away from Hawke, gingerly touching her bruised hip, then suddenly remembering what she'd been doing. She glanced at him just once and

turned quickly away. Her nervous fingers
opened the sliding doors of the picture
window where steps led down to the
beach.

"Excuse me," she murmured over her
shoulder, "I think I need some air."

She darted down the steps, embarrassed, and onto the gritty sand of the
beach, feeling it fill her sandals as she
started running along the shoreline. The
sun hovered low on the horizon, and the
breeze felt good in her face, cool and sobering. Her hair lifted from her hot neck,
cooling the dampness, bringing her sway-
ing mind slowly back into focus.

She was so lost in sensation that she
didn't notice how deserted the surroundings were or that a sand dune hid the
lonely stretch of beach from the house.
She didn't even hear the heavy thud of
footsteps behind her, or see the husky,
very angry man who was every bit as
quick as she was.

He caught up with her at the water's

edge, throwing her off-balance so that she fell heavily to the wet sand beside him. He turned, pinning her down, his strong hands pushing her wrists into the sand while the surf lathered around them, cold and wet.

"Hawke...the water," she stammered. He was dynamite at close range. This man who was so familiar was at once strange and dangerous and wickedly exciting. She gaped up at him with the shock she was feeling plain in her amber eyes, a little unnerved by the feel of his massive chest bruising the softness of hers, the way that mat of curling dark hair where his shirt was unbuttoned felt against the skin her low-cut top left revealed. His eyes were like slate now, dark and glittering, narrowing slightly as he looked down at his captive.

"Did you think you were going to get away with it?" he demanded roughly. "My God, Siri, you can't incite a man like that and expect to walk away untouched!''

''I didn't...I didn't mean to, Hawke,'' she breathed. ''It must have been the rum, and I'm not used to it. I'm sorry...!''

His fingers tightened on her wrists as his head bent. ''So am I,'' he said in a deep, tight voice. ''But I can't turn it on and off. Just be still, little girl. Don't make it worse by fighting me.''

She caught her breath when she saw his eyes drop to her mouth. ''Hawke, don't...'' she pleaded half-heartedly.

''Haven't you ever wondered,'' he whispered roughly as his warm, hard mouth brushed against hers in the dim reddish sunlight, ''what it would be like with me?''

She tried to answer him, but her blood was singing from the slow, brief, expert kisses he was whispering across her trembling lips.

Her fingers hesitantly touched the dark

face above hers, exploring his forehead, his cheek rough with its day's shadow of beard, his chiseled mouth—liberties she'd never have dared to take before, but he didn't seem to mind.

"Your hands are cold," he murmured.

"I...I'm nervous," she admitted.

His lips brushed against her closed eyelids. "It's a public beach," he reminded her. "This is hardly the place for what you're afraid I'm going to do to you."

"I know."

His teeth nipped at her lower lip. "Then why these little tremors I can feel going through you?" he asked in a deep, slow whisper.

"Hawke..."

His big hands slid beneath her shoulders, bringing her body sensuously up against him while his fingers caressed the softness of her back under the thin blouse.

"Stop talking," he murmured. "Touch me."

She relaxed unsteadily, pressing her small hands against his hard, cool chest, enjoying the masculine feel of it against the palms of her hands. His mouth explored hers very gently, coaxing, rather than forcing, her lips to part under the eager pressure of his.

"Hawke...the water," she whispered, feeling it dampen the back of her head.

"To hell with the water." His lips brushed against hers more insistently, pressing them apart until he could fit his mouth precisely to hers in a leisurely, ardent kiss that made a moan break from her throat.

His big hands slid up to her head, cradling it from the water, as his mouth grew hard and bruising and intimate in its assault on her soft lips.

"Don't..." she protested weakly, trying to escape his mouth as he began to deepen the kiss, to arouse feelings beyond her slight experience.

He drew back a breath to look down into her wide, amber eyes. "Why not?" he asked quietly.

"I...I've never kissed anyone...like that," she faltered.

"You're going to kiss me like that. Just relax," he whispered, tenderly smoothing the wild, damp hair away from her flushed face as he bent again. "There's a first time for everything, sparrow," he murmured against her mouth. "It's part of growing up, of being a woman. I want to be the one to teach you. Here, Siri. Now..." He forced her head back against his big hands, coaxing, tantalizing, teasing her soft mouth until he made her want it, need it, until her lips parted for him without protest and she sank down into the sand under the staggering wave of emotion that swept over her. A sound—half surprised gasp, half sob—wrenched from her.

"Does it make you ache, baby?" he whispered against her mouth.

"Yes!" she moaned, her nails biting into his shoulders as his body shifted slowly, sensuously against hers.

"Now you know how I felt in the beach house, you damned little tease!" he growled.

All at once, he rolled away from her and got to his feet. He stood facing the ocean, fumbling in his shirt pocket for a cigarette and match, and she thought just for an instant that she saw a shudder run through his big, husky body.

The blazing orange colors on the horizon danced around them, in a silence made noisy by the watery crash of the surf. The fiery glow gave Hawke a satanic look, emphasizing his darkness in a silhouette of power and strength against the horizon.

Siri sat up, aware of the dampness of her hair and back, and the bruised ache of her body from the fierce pressure of his. She tasted blood on her lips as she touched the inside of them with her tongue. The taste of him was there as well—a smoky, masculine taste that brought the color into her cheeks when she remembered how intimately she'd let him kiss her. As if that hadn't been bad enough, she'd revealed what his touch could do to her. She felt vaguely ashamed of herself, humiliated. If the name of the game was get even, he'd done a good job.

She got to her feet, still dazed. "I... I'm going back to the beach house," she managed weakly.

"You might as well, honey, the lesson's over," he said with a cutting edge on his deep voice. "I'm a little old to be tutoring curious teenagers, Siri. From now on, you'll have to let Holland teach you what you want to know. I'm not going to let you get to me like that again."

Get to him? Lessons? She felt all the color drain out of her face as she looked at him.

Six

He turned, as if he sensed her puzzlement, and she could feel his eyes touching her. His cigarette glowed orange in the fading light. "Isn't that clear enough?" he asked harshly. "Get out of my sight, you little hypocrite! Whatever the game is, I'm damned well not playing!"

Her hand went to her cheek, feeling as if he'd slapped her. She turned and started back toward the beach house alone.

With her heart pounding in her ears, she joined the others, trying not to let the turmoil of her emotions show. Her amber eyes had an unnatural brightness, and her hair was damp in back from the surf and disheveled from Hawke's rough fingers. But she managed to keep her voice calm, her hands steady.

"Where is Hawke?" Angel asked with venomous curiosity. "He followed you out."

"I don't know," Siri replied innocently. "He passed me on the beach and kept right on walking."

"I'll bet that did a lot for your ego," Kitty teased lightly.

Siri smiled. "It's not like that at all. Hawke's years too old for me. Goodness, he used to drive me to cheerleading practice when I was barely in my teens." She laughed, and saw some of the suspicion and tension drain out of Angel's delicately boned face.

"We will wait for him," the little Latin woman said. "In the meantime, let us have another drink."

Siri welcomed the rum punch as never before. Perhaps she could recover before...

Even as the thought formed in her mind, Hawke came in the door, looking as imperturbable as ever and just a little dangerous. His eyes darted toward Siri for just an instant before he joined Angel at the bar and after a while, the din of conversation dispelled some of Siri's tension. Not that the meal had much taste when they sat down to eat it. It might have been cardboard for all she knew. She kept her eyes on her plate and carried bites of food automatically to her mouth, pausing only to murmur appropriate responses to Kitty's bubbly remarks. The evening passed agonizingly slowly, a mingling of soft music and conversation that seemed to go forever.

Finally, Randy announced that he and Kitty had to get back to their hotel. Siri was right behind them, hoping that Hawke might decide to remain with Angel. But he didn't. Parrying aside her invitation to spend the day with her tomorrow, he explained that he'd be leaving town in the morning, adding that he'd look her up the next time he was passing through.

Siri followed the Hallers outside, while Angel took her sweet time saying goodbye to Hawke. Oh, why couldn't he have stayed? She didn't want to have to go back to that lonely suite with him, to be taunted anymore, to be shamed anymore. She just wanted to go back to Atlanta, and her father, and the newspaper. This was like being left in an unescapable cage with a lion.

Driving back to Panama City was the most uncomfortable thing in Siri's recent memory. She sat as far away from Hawke as possible, and her face was turned toward the darkness outside, with its sparse highlights of neon signs and colored lights as the "Miracle Strip" stretched out before them. The other two made casual conversation, but Hawke's replies were clipped and terse.

If only, Siri thought unhappily, they'd gone to see the awful snakes. She'd have had nightmares, but perhaps they wouldn't have been so painful. In her mind, she could see those dark, narrowed eyes looking down at her, feel the angry crush of his mouth, the bruising strength of his big body pressing hers relentlessly into the soft, damp sand.

She trembled just at the memory, wrapping her arms tight around her body to contain the shudder of shame that racked her. Why did she have to drink the rum? Why did she have to tease him like that while they were dancing? For all that she'd dreamed with a juvenile curiosity what it would be like to kiss him, it hadn't in any way prepared her for what had actually happened. She hadn't known that a man could be so demanding, that her own strength was nothing when compared with a man's superior force. She hadn't realized that a kiss could be so intimate, or that she could want it so much. Her eyes closed in embarrassment. He'd made her want it deliberately, but not because he wanted it to be a beautifully shared emotion. He had only wanted to pay her back for dancing a little too close.

They were at the hotel before she realized it. She stuck to Kitty like glue, finding one excuse after the other to keep her talking about art, about recipes, about anything. When the Hallers invited them in for a nightcap, Siri refused quickly. Pleading a headache, she asked Hawke if she could have the key; only to be shattered when he remarked casually that he'd go along, too. He silenced her protest with a look that knocked the resistance right out of her.

Meekly, she said her goodnights and followed him along to the suite they shared, waiting silently while he unlocked the door. She went in past him and reached for the doorknob at her bedroom.

"Siri." Just one word, just her name, but it was enough to freeze her where she stood.

She kept her eyes on the brass metal knob. "Please, just let me go to bed," she said in a voice totally unlike her normal tone. "You can't possibly make me feel any more ashamed than I already do."

"Did I hurt you?" he asked quietly.

She shook her head, flushing at the intimacy of the question, determined not to let him see the tears that were collecting in her eyes.

He took a long, agitated breath. "Since you're too afraid to listen to me, when you get home, ask Jared what that kind of provocation does to a man. It might surprise you. Goodnight, Siri.''

She stayed where she was until she heard the door open and close. She went quickly into her bedroom and locked the door behind her.

''Goodnight, Hawke,'' she whispered to the empty room.

The next morning, Siri found a note propped up on the coffee table written in Hawke's broad, scrawling hand.

''Siri,'' it began, ''if you need to contact me for any reason, I'll be at this number,'' and it gave an unfamiliar set of digits. ''I should be back by Thursday. Behave yourself. Hawke.''

She sighed, reading it. That last remark was just like him. Behave yourself, indeed! And just who did he think he was, anyway? Her keeper?

She stormed out of the suite and down to the beach. Well, she asked herself, what did she expect, a love letter? She blushed at the memory of that scene on the beach. It was a blessing not to have to face him for a few days. The wound was still too raw for the sting she'd feel every time she met those dark, knowing eyes. Only a few more days, she told herself. Only a few more days, and she could go back to her old familiar routine and pick up the pieces. But those pieces wouldn't include Mark. Not now. After what she'd discovered in Hawke's arms, it would be impossible to let Mark touch her ever again. She wondered miserably if she'd ever be able to feel that kind of emotion with anyone else.

Hawke was suddenly a stranger; a mature, very capable man who possessed a hidden fire she'd only dreamed he might conceal under the restrained impassive mask he wore. The man who'd wrestled her to the sand and kissed her with such bruising hunger—had that really been the Hawke who had brought her souvenirs from his travels and helped her with her homework? The idea took a lot of getting used to. She'd never experienced Hawke in any kind of real physical sense until now. She had a feeling she'd never quite get over it. He'd only been gone a few hours, and already she felt as if part of her had gone with him. That, too, was new—the feeling of being cut in two parts without someone.

Why did she miss him so much? Why couldn't she remember only the harsh words, the accusations he'd made, instead of the feel of that hard, sensual mouth as he'd made her yield to him? Was he really investigating a case, or was he using the case as an excuse to spend a few days with one of his women?

She dived into the waves and relished the feel of the cold water on her burning skin. She simply wouldn't think about it anymore. She wouldn't allow it!

Kitty came to see her that night, moaning that Randy had gone out somewhere with one of his friends and left her there all alone. Over coffee, they compared notes about Panama City and the delights of the beach.

"Will you get mad at me if I ask you what was wrong with Hawke last night?" Kitty asked suddenly, cupping her hands around the mug filled with steaming black coffee.

Siri looked down at her lap. "We... had an argument."

"Which Hawke started, no doubt." Kitty smiled. "I know Hawke very well. He was engaged to a friend of mine back in Charleston, just before he went into partnership with your father. I'm afraid she left him with a bad opinion of women in general. People tried to tell him that Nita liked to collect men, but..." She sighed softly, meeting Siri's intent, curious gaze. "Nita was just eighteen when she and Hawke started going together; a very young eighteen. She was very pretty, and I always felt she was flattered by the attentions of a man as masculine and mature as Hawke. But while he wanted commitment, she wanted variety and fun. What happened was inevitable.''

Siri was sitting on the edge of her seat. ''What did happen?'' she asked.

''To make a long story short, Hawke caught her out with a boy just a year older than she was. He broke the engagement, but I don't think he ever really got over it. And then, to have his mother found dead in her lover's apartment barely two weeks later...'' Kitty shook her head. ''He hasn't had an easy life. He had to let his law practice go while he straightened out the family finances. His father was too busy with women to be of much help.''

Siri was taking it all in with wide, astonished eyes. She'd known Hawke for so long, and not really known anything at all about him, it seemed.

''You didn't know, did you?'' Kitty probed gently.

Siri shook her head. "Hawke's very tight-lipped about his private life. I doubt even Dad knows very much about him." She sipped her coffee. "The girl he was engaged to...did he love her?"

"He was besotted with her, to use an old phrase. Nita was a gorgeous girl, and she wasn't ever intentionally cruel, just thoughtless. But even though I liked her, I wasn't blind to her faults. She was a born flirt, and she liked rich men. Hawke was good-looking, and had more money than even she could plow through very fast."

"Did she marry the boy?" Siri asked.

"Yes. As a matter of fact, she's gone through three husbands since, and I hear she's on the prowl for number four right now." Kitty shook her head. "Hawke had a lucky escape. I'm glad he left Charleston when he did. Nita wasn't quite what he needs in a wife," she added bitterly.

"He doesn't need a wife now," Siri

said with a knowing smile. "Not as long as he's got women like Gessie and Angel following him around. Angel was lovely, wasn't she?"

"If you thought she was so pretty," Kitty asked slyly, "why did you spend so much time glaring at her?"

Siri shifted uncomfortably. "Her brother irritated me."

"He irritated Hawke, too." Kitty set down her cup and looked at the other girl intently. "Siri, I told you about Nita for a reason. He was so bitter about it, I don't think he'll let another woman get close. But he might hurt one very badly out of that bitterness. I've come to know you these past few days. I wouldn't like to see you hurt."

Siri felt the words go through her and fought to keep calm. "You're very kind, Kitty, but I told you…"

"You told me one thing," came the wise reply, "but I watched you dancing with Hawke at Angel's house. Siri, it's very hard to hide when you care that much.''

"I'd had a lot to drink,'' she protested.

"Not that much. Siri,'' she said gently, leaning forward to cover the younger woman's trembling hands with her own, "didn't you know that you were in love with him?''

Those words haunted her through the night. "Didn't you know you were in love with him?'' The question returned like a painted horse on a merry-go-round, passing in front of her over and over again as she lay awake in her bed.

That couldn't be true, could it? Not Hawke, of all people, not after all this time! After all, you didn't go around falling in love with people who were like part of the family. And besides, he was years too old for her; too old, too set in his ways, and far too possessive.

She'd laughed off Kitty's probing remark convincingly enough at the time but it wasn't so easy to laugh it off in the darkness. To be with him, to touch him, to listen quietly as he talked with her father—when had such commonplace things become so important? And why hadn't she seen it coming? Why hadn't she realized what was happening while there might have been time to do something about it?

One thing was certain; Hawke didn't feel that way about her. She could still see the fury in his eyes, hear the whiplash of his voice as he accused her of provoking him into kissing her. Had she, really? Or, perhaps, had he wanted to...?

She drew a deep, unsteady breath. That, she told herself, was pure conceit. A man like Hawke wouldn't look twice at a girl as young and innocent as she was. He liked women like Angel—sleek, sophisticated, women who weren't afraid of the consequences of their flirting.

It was unsettling to realize just how deeply Hawke's absence was beginning

to affect her. The next day, she barely
touched food. She alternated between lying on the beach and swimming. Later,
she contemplated her miserable state on
the balcony when the sun went down.
She and Kitty visited some of the nearby
restaurants just for a change, and pored
over shells and souvenirs in the little gift
shops. But nothing took her mind off
Hawke for very long. She hated her own
helplessness. She'd never been vulnera-
ble before, never been dependent on a
man for happiness. She hated that new
vulnerability. She wished with all her
heart that she'd stuck to her guns in the
first place and stayed home. She could be
working on a fire right now, or some controversy in the police department. She
could be where the action was, instead of
stuck here on a beach littered with tourists. She could be doing something else
beside mooning over Hawke.

The second night, she forced herself to

sit in the living room of the lonely suite with her small portable typewriter on the coffee table. Without much success, she tried to concoct a presentable summary of the Devolg murder.

She studied her notes without any real enthusiasm. In a city that was notorious for homicide, another murder wasn't that sensational. Not that she'd become hardened to the extent that she didn't feel compassion for the families of victims, but she'd covered so many.

As she stared at her notes, she came across the original news story she'd done on the murder. Datelined Atlanta, it read: *Justin Devolg, 49, of Oak Street, Atlanta, was found dead in his apartment this morning from stab wounds.*

Her eyes scanned the page, resting on the paragraph that read: *Inspector Long stated that no motive for the killing was readily apparent. The dead man had a large sum of cash in his wallet, but it was untouched. He was wearing a diamond* *ring with an estimated value of $2,000 at the time of his death, and the ring was still on his finger when police arrived on the scene.*

A search is still pending for the un-identified man who fled when the body was discovered. Police have arrested a fifteen year old juvenile for questioning in connection with the murder, but no further information was available. The murder is still under investigation by lo-cal police and the FBI. Some pieces of evidence have already been sent to the state crime lab for inspection, and an early wrap-up of the case is expected by law enforcement officials.

Siri frowned. Of course, the update would confirm stab wounds as the cause of death, but they also would include the arrest of Hawke's young client in con-nection with the murder. The sensational nature of the case made it a natural for front page treatment.

She was searching her brain for a

good, strong lead, when the door opened unexpectedly and Hawke walked in. She gaped at him, as if she were looking at a ghost, her mind still on the murder.

"Have you eaten?" he asked quietly. "Or does the creative effort really take the place of food?"

"Sometimes it has to," she replied with a smile she didn't feel. She dragged her eyes away from him, hating the sudden quick beating of her heart as it reacted to the sight and sound of him. She was just now realizing how lonely she'd been these past few days, and how much she'd missed him. She felt a glow inside, as if a rainbow of warmth had suddenly raced through her.

"That doesn't answer my question," he reminded her.

"Oh, sorry," she apologized, "my mind was still on the Devolg story. No, I haven't eaten."

"Throw on a sweater and we'll walk

down the road to the seafood place," he told her. "It's a little chilly for summer."

"All right."

As excited as a teenager on her first date, she darted into her bedroom to change. She threw on a beige wraparound skirt and a green blouse. She ran a comb through her unruly hair. She left off makeup, except for a light touch of lipstick, and grabbed for her sweater as she went out the door into the living room.

Hawke was waiting for her at the main door. He was wearing a pale blue shirt that was open at the neck. Matched with his darker sports jacket, the outfit gave him a sophisticated look that went well with his masculine attractiveness. Her eyes absorbed the sight, dwelling on the broad, muscular sweep of his shoulders. Why did he have to be so good to look at, she wondered miserably, following him out into the hall. Why couldn't he have been fat and squatty with a face like a toad?

He caught the back of her neck, giving it an affectionate squeeze as they walked outside the hotel behind a group of tourists into the chill night air.

"What are you brooding about, honey?" he asked gently.

She almost told him. It very nearly slipped out, but she caught herself just in time.

"I'm just tired," she said quickly. "Kitty and I hit every tourist shop within walking distance this afternoon."

"You like her, don't you?" he asked.

She nodded and smiled. "I never had a sister, but if I could pick my own, I'd choose Kitty."

He was extremely quiet as the crowd of tourists moved a little ahead of them going down the side of the road while cars jammed together in a steady stream on the highway.

"How much did she tell you?" he asked suddenly, his eyes narrow and glittering as he glanced down at her.

"About what?" she asked uneasily.

"You damned well know about what," he growled.

She jerked her eyes away from his to the colorful neon lights ahead. He hadn't been back a half hour, and already he was trying to pick a fight.

She stopped and turned toward him. "Why don't I go back to the hotel and order my supper from room service?" she asked quietly. "At least that way we'll both be able to enjoy what we're eating."

He stared down at her long and hard. Finally, his hand came up and touched her cheek gently. "I'm being unreasonable, is that what you're trying to tell me?"

"Yes," she admitted.

"Oh, Siri," he said gently, "don't you know why? Aren't you even that sophisticated?"

She looked up at him, puzzled. "Trying to understand you is like trying to read Sanskrit,'' she observed. ''Hawke, what do you want?''

''You, damn it!'' he said curtly.

She flushed and turned away.

''Let's eat something,'' he said tightly, catching her by the arm as he began to walk again. ''Maybe it'll improve my temper.''

She felt shaken, uneasy. Was that why he'd begun to cut at her so much since they came on this trip—because of a purely physical attraction he couldn't help or do anything about? It made sense, it really did. But what a blow it was to her pride, to be desired only for the arrangement of physical features. It was as if he couldn't see her as a person at all. And didn't care to.

He led her into the seafood restaurant and seated her in one of the colorful red booths beside him. It created an intimacy that she could have done without. She couldn't move without touching him.

The waitress brought ice water and menus, and they studied them silently.

"I'd like the scallops," she said finally, handing him the menu as the waitress came back, "and coffee."

He ordered for both of them, automatically reaching for a cigarette when the waitress went away.

"Will the smoke bother you?" he asked, glancing down at her.

She shook her head. Her hands were wrapped around her water glass as if it were a life jacket, keeping her head above water.

He caught a strand of her hair and tugged it gently, forcing her frightened eyes up to his. He read them, and smiled.

"I'm not going to do anything about it," he said softly, reading the thought in her mind. "You're perfectly safe, little bird."

She looked into his eyes. "I'm sorry for what I did at the beach house," she said in a subdued tone. "It really was the rum. I'd never have done anything like that if I'd been myself.''

His dark brows came together. ''You've never tried to interest a man like that before?'' he asked.

''I haven't and I wouldn't,'' she replied. ''It's cheap and cruel.''

''It depends on who's doing it, and for what reason,'' he said softly. ''I said things to you that I shouldn't have, and I regret them. But I've never lost my head with a woman before. It shook me.''

The admission startled her. ''But you didn't…!''

He tugged the strand of hair again, more firmly. ''I very nearly didn't let you go,'' he said solemnly. ''It was good, Siri. It was so damned good, I didn't want to stop. I was rougher with you than I ever meant to be, and more intimate. It must be my age,'' he laughed mirthlessly. ''I've never stooped to the attempted seduction of innocents before. And I'm going to take you home tomorrow before I try it again. You're very...vulnerable where I'm concerned, Siri,'' he remarked with a scowl. ''It's damned flattering, but extremely dangerous. One thing I told you I meant—you need to learn about adult relationships with a boy your own age. I'm too old and jaded to teach you in any respectable way. In short, little one,'' he added with a mocking smile, ''I want it all. Not just nibbles.''

She blushed, dropping her eyes to the shiny table where her reflection looked back at her. ''I shouldn't have come.''

''It's my own fault, baby. I talked you into it.'' He leaned back to light his cigarette, only to have to put it out again as the waitress reappeared with two full plates of scallops, tossed salads, rolls, and baked potatoes.

''Don't dwell on it, sparrow,'' Hawke told her with a quiet smile. ''Tomorrow we'll be home. You'll be back on the job, and swinging at Holland, and all this will seem like a dream.''

"Or a nightmare?" she teased with a little of her old impudence as she glanced at him.

"I wouldn't go that far," he said with a considering look. "You left some pretty deep marks on my shoulders."

She blushed to the roots of her hair and gasped unconsciously at the reference. She attacked her scallops with a vengeance, ignoring the soft, amused laughter at her ear.

It was all a game to him, she thought as she ate. Just a game to play with her, and he was a master at it. She wasn't experienced enough to laugh it off, or throw the taunting remarks back at him. Oh, I wish I was five years older, Hawke Grayson, she thought angrily. I'd pay you back with interest, if I had just a little more experience under my belt!

They walked back to the hotel in companionable silence. Siri didn't dare break it, for fear that he'd start teasing her again, and she didn't think she could bear it.

In one way, it would be good to go back home and leave the danger of being with him like this behind. In another sense, it was going to be horribly painful. Now that she finally knew how she felt about the broad-shouldered, husky man at her side, it was going to be all that much harder to go back to the old routine. Having had a taste of heaven, life was going to be very boring for a long time, maybe forever. She glanced up at him, her eyes resting briefly, involuntarily, on the chiseled curve of his mouth. Why couldn't he have been ten years younger? Why couldn't she have been ten years older?

They were alone in the elevator going up to their suite, and she felt his eyes on her every foot of the short climb. He got to the door first and opened it for her, standing aside to let her enter. She started for her bedroom, as she usually did when they came home late. The last time, she thought, this was the last time....

"Siri..." he called gently.

She turned slowly, her sad amber eyes meeting his across the short distance that separated them. His were dark and strange, smoldering.

"Infatuation dies a natural death when it doesn't have anything to feed on," he said. "And that's all it is, sparrow. You're growing up fast. I've taught you things you should have learned in easy stages, and it's gone to your head, that's all. Don't mistake it for something more permanent."

She felt absolutely whipped. Was that what it seemed like to him, a teenage infatuation? Did he think her such a child?

"I...I didn't say..." she faltered, embarrassed.

He jammed his hands into his pockets, his eyes narrowing. "You didn't have to say it. It's written all over you, every time you look at me."

Seven

She bit her lip, staring down at her toes peeking out of the sandals, feeling the lump come into her throat.

"As you say," she managed unsteadily, "it's just a…phase I'm going through. It doesn't mean…anything."

There was a muffled curse. "If you keep looking like that, I'm going to carry you over to the sofa and make love to you, Siri! I want you so much, it's like a fire burning inside me, and damn it, you're not helping!''

Her eyes jerked up incredulously to his dark, heavily lined face. The sight of him made her knees go weak. Would it be so very wrong to give in? To feel that hard, hungry mouth on hers just once more, to yield to arms so much stronger than her own...

"You'd let me love you, wouldn't you, little girl?'' he asked in a deep, low whisper.

Her lips trembled as they formed the words. "Hawke, I...'' she began huskily.

But before she could get them out, the insistent jangle of the phone broke into the silence like an air raid siren. She flinched at the sound.

Hawke turned on his heel and went to answer it. Siri moved out onto the balcony, letting the sea breeze cool her burning skin, settle the throbbing nerves that screamed from disappointment. Through the clearing fog of her emotions, she heard Hawke's deep, curt voice in the distance as he spoke into the receiver.

Minutes passed before he joined her on the balcony. He didn't speak at first, not until he'd halfway smoked a cigarette.

"That was my housekeeper in Charleston," he said. "The overseer had a heart attack this afternoon. I'll have to fly up there and make arrangements for someone to take over the farm until he's back on his feet."

"Oh, I'm sorry," she murmured.

"You've never been to Charleston, have you?" he asked suddenly.

Her heart jumped. "No, I haven't."

"Come with me, Siri."

She hesitated, remembering what had almost happened once before. What if...?

"We'll take the Hallers with us," he said quietly. "I think...we could use a chaperone, don't you?"

"Yes," she managed in a whisper.

He drew a deep breath. "I ought to

send you home," he said. "You know that, don't you?"

"I know," she replied.

"But you don't really want to go any more than I want to let you," he added roughly. "I missed you like hell, Siri!"

She turned, her eyes seeking his in the soft light from the living room. It was magic! Sheer magic! Did he care, could he?

He moved away from her, back into the living room. "I think you'd better go to bed," he said.

She followed him into the living room. One look at the set of his jaw was enough to tell her not to argue with him. For all the emotion there'd been in his voice in the darkness, there wasn't a trace of it on his face.

She wanted to ask him...but she didn't dare. She nodded quietly and turned toward her bedroom. Just before she fell asleep, she realized he'd told her nothing about his trip.

* * *

The next morning, with Randy and
Kitty in the back seat of the big Cessna,
they were on the way to Charleston.
Hawke's handyman, Charles Simms, met
them at the airport outside Charleston in
a spacious Lincoln town car and drove
them to the farm, which was only
minutes away.

Siri watched her surroundings change
minute by minute with a bubbling fascination. Charleston was a city of many
different faces; it ranged from gorgeous
white beaches to cobblestoned streets,
where flower vendors and basket-weavers
plied their trade; from two-hundred year
old homes to modern skyscrapers. Palm
trees and crepe myrtle mingled naturally
in this city once called Charles Town.

"Looking for the cannons?" Hawke
teased as he saw Siri glancing out toward
the ocean. "I'll make time to carry you
out to Fort Sumter and Fort Moultrie
while we're here."

"I'd like that," she said enthusiastically. "Can I fire off a cannon?"

"I don't think the city fathers would like that," he replied.

She sighed. "I never get to have any fun."

The family estate was called Graystone, and once they followed the winding, flower-laced driveway up to the main house, she understood why. The house was built from pale gray stone in a Gothic design, with a soaring portico and columns placed in pairs on either side. A balcony curved over the portico, with black wrought-iron railings, and fourth floor over-portico windows completing the Gothic styling. It was a large house, but not massive like some of the residences they'd passed going through the city. It was impressive without being gaudy.

For Siri, as she stepped out of the car and looked around at the neatly kept grounds, at the massive oaks with their beards of Spanish moss, at the river beyond the garden, there was a sense of belonging. It was strangely like coming home after a long absence. And when she turned and met Hawke's intent gaze, the feeling was complete.

The three of them were introduced to Mr. Simms' wife, Mary, who'd kept house at Graystone ever since Mr. Hawke was a lad. She was a buxom woman with gray hair neatly coiled at the back of her head, and Siri had a feeling that she could set a table like no one else.

As they climbed the steps to the wide, immaculately scrubbed portico, Siri noted the big rocking chairs and settees that lined the walls. In the distance, the soft watery sound of the river could be heard along with the swish of the tree limbs touching and the mingled birdsongs. It was like something out of another world; a bower of peace in the world full of turmoil.

"Oh, Hawke, it's heaven," she murmured as they went into the house behind the Hallers.

"It can be lonely," he remarked quietly.

She met his dark eyes. "Any place can be."

Hawke gave them a grand tour, and Siri was flooded with impressions of an elliptical stairway, curved walls, rounded banisters of pure mahogany, and large paintings of previous owners of the house.

"Graysons have lived here for over 200 years," Kitty told Siri, as they followed along behind the men. "In Hawke's den, there's a portrait of the first owner, with a bayonet tear in the center of it. They say a Union soldier used it for target practice when federal troops camped here during the Civil War."

"You and Randy have been here before, haven't you?" Siri asked.

"It was a long time ago," Kitty replied

softly, and Siri knew somehow that it had been when Hawke's mother died.

When the luggage was arranged in their rooms, and they'd had a light lunch, they got the tour of the farm. Hawke walked beside Siri, his arm brushing against hers as they first went to the big barn, where a prize polled Hereford bull pranced proudly in a paddock surrounded by a white fence.

"Gray's Fancy," Hawke mused, gesturing toward the huge animal. "The pride of my stock, and he knows it. He's sired five champions already."

Siri cocked her blond head at him. "He does have a macho look about him," she observed.

"You'd have the same look if you carried the price tag he does." Randy laughed. "That's a very expensive ton of beef."

"Don't say that," Kitty cautioned, "you'll hurt his feelings!"

The next stop was the spacious stretch

of green pasture where the polled Hereford main herd dotted the countryside with their red and white coats. Siri leaned back against the white rail fence and watched them moving lazily back and forth against a horizon of trees.

"The farm covered two counties over a century and a half ago," Hawke told her, while he smoked a cigarette. "Now there are barely a thousand acres left. We raise a few crops, but cattle are our main interest."

Siri gazed up at him. "You haven't been here in a long time, have you?" she asked, so softly that the Hallers, who were several yards away, wouldn't hear.

He studied the glowing tip of his cigarette. "No," he said finally, "I haven't wanted to come near the place until now."

"Could we see the gardens? I got a glimpse of them..."

"Come on." He caught her elbow and

turned her with him, calling to the Hallers to join them.

The gardens were on the banks of the Ashley River, amid towering magnolia and expansive oak trees with curling lavender-gray strands of Spanish moss trailing down from their lofty branches. The mixing of colors was perfect; the white and pink of the hydrangeas, the violet crepe myrtle, the white snowball bushes, and the pale purple wisteria hanging like grape flowers. It was enough to take an artist's breath away.

"You should see it in the spring," Kitty sighed, "when the magnolias are blooming along with the dogwoods and rose bushes. It's a symphony of color."

"It must be lovely," Siri murmured, her eyes on the lazy current of the river as it wound through the cypress trees at its banks. "What a lovely place to have a picnic."

Hawke turned on his heel, his face taut. "We'd better be getting back. I've got some calls to make about a temporary overseer."

Siri hung behind with Kitty. She knew that Hawke was remembering happier times by the river—maybe picnics he'd shared with Nita in his younger days. She felt a twinge of envy at the thought of how much he must have loved Nita.

Hawke found two possible replacements for his ailing manager before sundown, leaving the interviews to do the next day.

The four of them sat down to a seafood supper that Hawke swore was Mary's crowning accomplishment—stuffed crab and lobster tails. It was the best Siri could remember ever having, but she'd never eaten in surroundings this elegant. Crystal chandeliers hung overhead and old silver utensils and serving dishes adorned the table. It brought the distance between Hawke and her into vivid focus. Looking down the table at him, sitting so majes-

tically at the end of the table in a dark
suit, she understood him just a little better. The rugged aristocrat. The plantation
master. He'd have been right at home in
the nineteenth century.

After the last of the crab was gone,
they went into the parlor for after dinner
drinks. Siri accepted a small glass of delicately aged French brandy, and sneaked
away at the first opportunity to sit in one
of the big rocking chairs on the porch
outside.

The atmosphere of night in this se-
cluded green paradise was delicious.
They were far removed from traffic and
the smell of car exhaust. Siri sipped her
brandy quietly, drinking in the serenity
around her; the low murmur of the river,
and the soft chirp of crickets in the thick
woods around the house.

"You've got the makings of a country
girl," Hawke said at her shoulder.

"Would you rent me about six cubic

inches of this and have it mailed to my house?'' she asked with a smile.

''You'd miss the sirens after the second week,'' he replied, taking the chair next to hers.

''Where are Randy and Kitty?'' she asked.

''On the phone. Kitty wanted to call her mother while she was in town.''

''Don't she and Randy still live in Charleston?'' she asked.

''No. They have a home in Savannah now.'' He sipped his whiskey and leaned back in his rocking chair with a heavy sigh. ''Mary has a way with crab,'' he murmured.

''Mary has gifted hands,'' she agreed. ''Hawke, I never did get to ask you what you discovered about that witness.''

''I found him,'' he replied.

She sat straight up in her chair. ''Where? Who is he? Will he testify? Did he…?''

He chuckled heartily. "For God's sake, one question at a time!"

"All right," she agreed breathlessly. "Will he testify?"

"He'll testify."

"Do you know who killed Devolg?" she persisted, leaning across the arm of her rocking chair to intently study his impassive face.

"I think so."

"Are you going to tell me?" she burst out while he emptied his glass in one swallow. He set the glass down on the floor and leisurely lit a cigarette.

He glanced at her with one eyebrow raised. "And make you an accessory?" he asked with mock incredulity.

"Hawke!" she groaned. "You know I can keep a confidence, and you know I wouldn't write anything until you tell me to!"

He smiled at her eagerness. "Remember I told you that Davy Megars had an older sister?"

"Your client Davy?"

"The same. Well, she had a boyfriend, a very jealous boyfriend who knew she was making time with Devolg." He leaned back in his chair and watched the path of a cricket as it crawled jerkily off the porch. "I had a feeling Davy was protecting someone. Youngsters don't generally go around killing other men without a motive. And the fact that his fingerprints were found in Devolg's room only placed him at the scene, they didn't prove he was the murderer."

"What would he have been doing there?" she asked, her mind nowhere near as sharp as Hawke's.

"Getting his sister out," he replied.

She blinked at him. "You think Davy's sister did it?"

"She had the best motive, from the information I've gathered. Devolg was a known womanizer, and he liked variety. Davy's sister has a nasty, jealous temper.

All I need is to get her on the stand for five minutes. I can break her.''

It was the way he said it, the confidence in his deep, slow voice, the hardness of his face, that made her certain he could do exactly that. She studied him in the muted light of the porch, her eyes tracing his profile lovingly as he suddenly turned and caught the look in her eyes.

''What are you thinking, Siri?'' he asked quietly.

''That I hope you never get me on the stand,'' she said with a nervous laugh. She finished the brandy and set her own glass down beside the rocking chair.

He turned in his chair to face her, catching the side of her neck with his big, warm hand to hold her eyes level with his, as she raised back up. ''I'd never hurt you,'' he told her. ''Not on the witness stand, or in any place on earth.''

Her pulse ran wild at the slow, caressing touch of his fingers. She looked into

his eyes, and everything she'd ever
wanted was within the reach of her arms.

"Woman," he whispered huskily, "I
didn't mean for this to happen. But, I
need you..."

He gently tilted her face and reached
across the scant inches that separated
them to touch his mouth lightly to hers.
She caught her breath as he increased the
pressure, shifting his hand to the nape of
her neck to force her closer.

"God, it's not enough!" he said in a
rough whisper. He moved suddenly, ris-
ing to lift her out of the rocking chair, his
mouth claiming hers again as he crushed
her body against his, burning all thought
of protest out of her whirling mind. She
locked her arms around his neck, strain-
ing closer, returning the fervor of his
kisses without reserve.

She felt him drop back down into his
own chair, carrying her with him. He
draped her over his knees, allowing her
head to fall weakly back into the crook

of his arm, as he looked down at her with eyes laden with passion.

His chest rose and fell unsteadily against her soft, yielding body, but for all the passion in his eyes, his face was like chiseled rock. Her own breath came quickly, unsteadily, and her lips trembled as she stared back at him.

Sanity returned all in a rush. She vividly remembered the last time he'd kissed her, and what he'd said to her. She had made up her mind that he wasn't going to hurt her again like that.

"May I get up now?" she asked in a rusty whisper. "You...you said last time that you were through giving me lessons."

Something came and went in his eyes, but he erased the hardness from his expression with a slow, lazy smile. "I don't think you need many more, do you?" he countered.

She lowered her eyes to his massive chest in the pure white shirt. "Why?"

she asked gently, and he knew she wasn't talking about "lessons."

"If you need a reason," he said quietly, "because of this." He caught one of her slender hands and pressed it palm down to his chest just above his heart. The beat was heavy and erratic. "Do you feel it, Siri?" he asked deeply.

She drew a shaky breath. "I...a lot of women must have affected you that way."

"A few." His own hand slid up from her waist to rest not quite intimately at the curve where her own heart was running wild. "I seem to have the same effect on you, sparrow."

"Don't make fun of me," she pleaded in a ghostly voice.

"I don't want to make fun of you. I want to make love to you," he said in a low, quiet voice that made shivers race down her spine.

"You know I've never..."

He laughed softly. "Maybe I'd better

clarify that, little innocent. I want to hold you, and kiss you, and touch you. I can do that without taking you into my bed," he whispered at her ear.

"Hawke Grayson, you are the most..."

His mouth brushed against hers slowly, tasting hers in a tender, leisurely encounter that instantly quieted her. Meanwhile, his thumb was tracing delicious patterns on the bodice of her dress, touching and lifting with a strange rhythm that made her tense with unknown sensations.

"You're tense," he murmured. "Are you afraid of me, or is it that good?"

"Hawke..." she protested weakly.

"Tell me, honey."

She twisted, trying to escape the maddening caress of his fingers, but the arm behind her gripped like steel and held her captive, and she moaned sharply, her nails digging involuntarily into his hard chest through the soft fabric.

His cheek slid against hers caressingly.

"Your nails are sharp, little cat," he murmured, a smile in his voice.

"I'm...sorry," she managed unsteadily, her eyes closing as she yielded, trusting him even against her will, drugged with pleasure.

"I'm not. Here." He unbuttoned the top three buttons of the silky shirt and slid her cool hand inside it. "Anything goes, Siri," he said quietly. "Anything."

"But...you said..." she faltered.

"To hell with what I said," he growled as his mouth opened on hers. "I want you."

Before she could react to the words, he was teaching her how agonizingly sweet a kiss could be, and she gave up trying to think.

The sound of voices made him raise his head. He looked searchingly down into her misty, amber eyes.

Her fingertips traced a tiny pattern on the warm, bronzed flesh of his chest through the mat of dark hair. "Are you trying to seduce me?'' she whispered lazily.

''Not yet,'' he murmured, ''but if you keep that up, I may damned well try.''

''Oh!'' she breathed. She withdrew her hand with a shaky sigh. ''Sorry.''

''You still don't know what you can do to me, do you?'' he asked quietly. ''You sweet, little witch, I step into an inferno every time you touch me.''

She searched his face quietly as the voices inside the house drew nearer. ''If it's any consolation, you do the same thing to me,'' she admitted.

''Any experienced man could, Siri,'' he told her. ''Don't let it go to your head.''

She dropped her eyes to his chest. ''I won't.''

''I like the taste of you,'' he said, holding her close for a moment, ''and the way you feel in my arms. But when we get back to Atlanta, nothing will have changed. Nothing, Siri, do you understand?''

She looked up and met his eyes solemnly. ''Dad always used to tell me to live one day at a time.''

There were shadows of some deep, private sadness in his eyes for just an instant. ''That's what I mean, sparrow. For the next two or three days, we'll forget the rest of the world and enjoy being with each other. But the minute I land that plane in Atlanta, I'm going to walk away from you. And I won't look back.''

She bit her lower lip. ''I...I won't have an affair with you, Hawke,'' she said self-consciously.

''You're damned right you won't,'' he said roughly. ''I told you before I wasn't going to play fast and loose with you, and I meant it. I won't promise not to kiss you, you impudent little minx, but it isn't going any further than that. I don't want your innocence on my conscience. I've got enough to haunt me without that.''

She shifted in his arms, feeling the tension drain out of her to be replaced with a strange, easy comradeship. "Does that mean," she asked, "that I have to promise not to seduce you, either?"

He grinned down at her. "It's only fair. But would you know how?"

"I'm learning. In a few years, look out."

"My God, you'll be devastating," he agreed. He leaned back in the chair and pulled a cigarette out of his pocket, holding it lightly in his fingers. "Will the smoke bother you? If you're going to mind it, you'll have to get up, because it's either this or a shot of whiskey."

She linked her hands behind his head. "Do I unnerve you, Mr. Grayson?" she asked with a smile.

"Yes, Madam," he replied, "you do."

She nuzzled her cheek against his jacket, loving the solidness, the warmth of his body, the deep sound of his voice in the darkness. He was, she thought drowsily, so easy to love.

To love. Her eyes flew open. She gazed across the breadth of his chest to the long porch with darkness at its end. She loved him. For the first time, she let herself admit it, feel it, drown in it. She loved Hawke. And what good was it going to do when he'd already told her how it was going to end? He wasn't a loving man. He could want a woman, true, but Siri wanted more than desire from him. She wanted a thousand nights like this one to lie in his arms listening to the night, and feel a security that had never been hers to enjoy until now, with this man. She wanted children with thick black hair and dark eyes. Her eyes closed. Behind her eyelids, she could feel the warmth of tears brewing.

The Hallers came out onto the porch unexpectedly, and Siri started and sat up. Hawke pulled her down again and held her with one big arm.

"Be still," he murmured over her head, "they're family."

"But you said..."

"Damn it, will you be quiet?" he growled. "Are you ashamed to be seen like this with me?"

"Oh, no!" she said involuntarily.

He smiled gently down at her, and the look in his dark eyes made her want to cry. "Then stop trying to escape. Just act naturally."

"How can I, when I've never been in a man's lap before?" she asked.

The smile broadened. "You felt right at home a few minutes ago," he reminded her.

She blushed. "Beast!"

"That isn't what you were whispering under your breath, either," he whispered as the Hallers came into view. "Come on out," he called to them before Siri could think of a reply. "I'm rocking my *'niece.'*"

"Is that true, Siri?" Kitty teased, a knowing smile on her face.

"No, it isn't," she replied. "He's trying to lead me into a life of sin."

"Don't look at me," Hawke protested nonchalantly. "You're the one holding me down," he added. "A man can't be left alone in safety these days. Brazen young women leaping onto his lap, attacking him..."

"And who attacked who?" Siri demanded.

"Whom," Hawke corrected. "I thought you were an accomplished journalist."

"Of all the..." she began.

"Where are we going tomorrow?" Randy broke in with a grin.

"That," Kitty interpreted, "is called a 'red herring,' in case you didn't know. In other words, time out!"

Siri laughed, relaxing in Hawke's loose grip. "Fair enough. Where are we going tomorrow?" she asked him.

"To Fort Sumter. I'll let you play with the cannons," he added.

"Will you stand in front of one while I play with it?" she asked coaxingly.

Randy and Kitty burst out laughing, as Hawke tried unsuccessfully to turn her over his knee.

It was a lovely, sunny day, and driving down the Battery on the way to Fort Sumter, the Atlantic had never looked bluer. Siri glanced at Hawke across the front seat, her eyes caressing the dark face and hair. He was wearing a red knit shirt with jeans, and she'd never seen him look more handsome. Her own white sundress emphasized her slenderness and her fairness. The contrast between them was striking. She paid so much attention to it that she missed most of the scenery between Graystone and the fort, and wasn't at all sorry.

Fort Sumter faced the ocean, a pale aging relic of an all but forgotten war. The big black cannons still stood guard over the harbor, but the fort's walls were little more than crumbling brick over which an American flag, not a Confederate one, flew proudly. She looked out to sea, feeling the wind in her face, absorbing the faint sea smell as she watched the seagulls in the distance. It was awesome to stand here where so much history had been made. It was impossible to be unaware of those who came before.

Fort Sumter was only one of many tourist attractions they made time to see. Siri's favorite by far was Magnolia Gardens, with its unbelievable number of flowering trees and shrubs, its links with the Civil War and England, and its legacy of almost unworldly beauty.

"It reminds me a little of Graystone," Siri remarked to Hawke, as they strolled over the famous little bridge.

"It should. My great-grandmother fell so much in love with it that her husband created a miniature garden in its image just to shut her up," he laughed.

Eight

The story made her curious, and when they got back to Graystone, she had to go back and stroll through the garden again.

Randy and Kitty borrowed the car to visit their relatives, leaving Hawke and Siri alone. He spent an hour or so with his new overseer before he joined her in the quiet garden, where she stood under one of the monstrous oaks that stood like sentinels beside the river.

He came up behind her, pulling her back against him with his arms locked securely around her small waist.

"What do you think of Graystone?" he asked.

Her fingers curled over his forearms, tangling in the dark, wiry hair. She sighed, letting her body go limp against his. "It's beautiful, Hawke," she said wistfully. "Like something out of a postcard book—colorful and peaceful."

"And lonely," he added quietly.

"Is that why you stayed away so long?" she asked.

His arms tightened, and she felt his warm, hard chest expand at her back. "The world was pretty black for me when I left here the last time. I'd just lost my fiancée—as Kitty told you, I'm sure. And my mother had just been buried. I could hardly bear the sight of this garden. She loved it so." He drew a deep breath. "I had to get away. Somehow it was easier to let Jackson run the farm for me.

Even when my father died, I only came home long enough for the funeral. This is the longest I've stayed since. It's also the first time I've been able to enjoy being here." His cheek nuzzled against hers. "You bring the color back into it for me, Siri."

"I'm glad," she murmured, smiling. "Do you think you'll ever come back here to live?"

His body went taut. "Why should I? The house is too big for one man, even with the staff."

"You could get married, raise a family," she said gently.

"In a little over a month, I'll be thirty-nine years old, little girl," he said quietly.

"Does that mean," she asked with mock denseness, "that your advanced age won't allow you to father children?"

"You damned little irritant," he chuckled. "What I mean is that, at my age, it's hard to tell if a woman wants me or access to my wallet.''

''Wear old gunny sacks and carry a dented cup around with you for a few weeks,'' she suggested, ''and you'll be able to weed out the ones that want you for yourself.''

''I thought Jared said he educated you. Where? At the funny farm?'' he asked.

She laughed softly. ''Do you really wonder about women?''

''Most men do.''

''I mean, about if they're after you because of what you can give them? You're...not an unattractive man,'' she said, faltering on the words.

''You've already shown me that,'' he said at her ear.

She flushed hotly, and drew in a quick, shaky breath. ''It's...it's very peaceful here. I like the sound of the river,'' she said enthusiastically.

''You're hedging,'' he said, and she

felt rather than saw the smile on his dark face. His arms tightened.

"Sometimes I think you enjoy embarrassing me more than winning cases," she accused.

"Yes, I do. You adorable brat, you wouldn't give a damn if I didn't have a dime, and I know it." He let her go. "But the timing is all wrong, Siri. We'd better get back. Mrs. Simms will have supper waiting."

"All right." She walked along beside him, enjoying the slow pace he set, enjoying the surroundings of the farm as dusk approached.

"Thank you for letting me come home with you," she said softly. "Everyone needs a green memory to take out and water when snow lies on the ground."

He bent his head to light a cigarette. "From now on, every time I come here, I'll see you," he said.

"Is that good or bad?"

"A touch of both," he admitted with

a lazy smile that didn't quite reach his eyes.

"Oh."

He caught her slender hand in his and pressed it gently. "Just enjoy today, Siri. Don't try to live your whole life in a day."

She locked her slender fingers with his broad, warm ones. "Do I do that?"

He smiled. "Constantly."

"I never pretended to be a patient person," she reminded him.

"It comes with age."

"Does it, Methuselah?" she asked with mock solemnity.

His eyes narrowed, his lips compressed. "Methuselah, did you say?" He jerked her body against his, wrestling with her in the shade of a gigantic oak, while she laughed and struggled with him playfully.

He caught the back of her head, holding it steady while he looked down at her. "Let me show you how old I am..." he

threatened, crushing his warm mouth
down on hers unexpectedly.

With a whisper of a sigh, she yielded
to him, her lips involuntarily parting to
invite a deeper caress.

He drew back instantly. "Not like
that," he whispered roughly. "It's like
striking a match to dry kindling."

She leaned back against his hard arms.
"I'm sorry," she said softly. "I...I'm not
very good at this."

"You're too good at it, honey," he
said, deadly serious. "Let's go."

She walked quietly beside him, disappointed and a little shaken by his sudden
withdrawal, and the hardness that returned to his dark face. He seemed to re-
sent even the small effect her nearness
had on him, as if he hated anything that
touched or threatened his near-perfect
self control. She sighed wistfully. Any
day now, it would be all over. They'd be
back in Atlanta, and things would be the
way they were before the trip began. She

studied the ethereal beauty of the estate
with eyes that longed for more than just
a passing acquaintance with it. How
lovely it would be to grow old here, with
Hawke....

Just as they reached the house, a silver
Mercedes pulled up in the driveway and
stopped. Hawke froze beside Siri as the
door opened and a tall, slender, strikingly
beautiful brunette stepped out of it with
a practiced grace. In her clinging white
dress and matching sandals, she was el-
egance personified.

"Hawke, how nice to see you again,"
the woman said softly, and Siri knew in
a blinding flash who she was.

"Hello, Nita," he replied with a pleasant smile. "It's been a long time."

"Too long," she said, batting her long
lashes up at him as she moved closer.
"Kitty's mother told me you were here.
I just had to see you."

"How's your husband?" he asked.

"I divorced him three months ago," she replied sweetly. "I've been so lonely..."

"Have you moved back to Charleston?" he asked.

"I'm thinking about it," she cooed. Her eyes darted to Siri, as if she'd just realized she was there. "Who's this?" she asked with a poisonous smile.

"My partner's daughter. Siri Jamesson, Nita Davis," he introduced them. "Kitty and Randy are with us on this trip."

"You'll be in town for a while, won't you?" the brunette asked hopefully.

"Until tomorrow," Hawke said, and Siri felt herself doing a double take. He hadn't mentioned that before.

"Please have dinner with me, Hawke," Nita pleaded with one silky hand caressing his arm. Her eyes were bright blue and extremely seductive. "For old time's sake?"

Siri imagined that he hesitated for just

a second before he answered her. "All right." He turned toward Siri, his face impassive, his dark eyes telling her nothing. "Don't wait supper. I'll be late."

"Oh, darling, it's been so long," Nita breathed as she led him back to the Mercedes.

He put her in on the passenger side and slid in under the wheel. Siri didn't wait to watch them drive off. She turned and went quickly into the house. If he'd needed to emphasize how little she meant to him, that was enough. She got the message.

Supper was quiet. The Hallers still hadn't come home, when Siri finished eating and went into the kitchen with Mrs. Simms to help the elderly woman with the dishes.

"Lass, I don't need help, you know," Mrs. Simms told her with a smile.

"I helped mess them up," Siri pointed out reasonably, "and it's only fair that I help clean up. Besides," she added with a grin, "I like the feel of warm soapy water. I never let Dad buy me an automatic dishwasher for that reason."

"A homebody, are you?" Mrs. Simms deftly washed plates and passed them across to be rinsed and dried. "No young man?"

Siri paused. "A friend," she corrected. "No one I want to marry."

"No one except that blind man who comes to visit me every year or so, is that it?" the older woman probed.

"Blind man...?"

"Mr. Hawke," came the bland reply. "Because if he can't see what's written all over you when he walks into a room, he has to be blind."

"He...he doesn't know," Siri said quickly. "He can't, not ever. He's already made it very clear that he doesn't have any interest in marriage or a family, and I've made it clear that I can't settle for anything less."

"Ah, a standoff." Mrs. Simms

laughed. "Not for long, though," she added with a sly, teasing glance. "I've seen the way he looks at you when you don't notice. It's as if his eyes touch you, lass. I've seen that look in a man's eyes too often to mistake it, but not since that baggage broke their engagement have I seen it in Mr. Hawke's eyes."

"Nita, you mean?" she asked, wiping the last of the plates dry.

"That baggage," Mrs. Simms repeated, "never cared for him, she never did. And now here she comes back like it's been days instead of years and carries him off again. Nothing stupider than a man. I thought he'd had better sense," she added vehemently. "She'll have him trapped again before he knows it, poor thing. You mark my words, men are too susceptible to a woman like that. She gets him so hungered that his mind breaks down. Aye, you can laugh, but it's what happens."

Siri drew a deep, sobering breath.

"Maybe that's what I should have done," she said with a wry grin, "but I don't know how."

"You look like you'd be a fast learner," Mrs. Simms teased. "And if you love the man, lass, it comes natural."

But what if the man doesn't love you? She thought it, but she didn't say it. Instead, she sang the praises of the Scotswoman's pudding, and went away with the secret recipe for it.

It was late evening when the Hallers came back, and Hawke still hadn't put in an appearance. Siri knew without being told that he and Nita weren't just talking all this time, and the pain caused tears to form in her eyes as she sat quietly on the porch listening to the night sounds. Had it only been last night that she'd been sitting here when Hawke reached for her and kissed her so passionately that the breath left her body? She drew a shaky sigh. What a bittersweet memory that was going to be.

Randy and Kitty came up the stairs running, laughing, and she envied them their lightheartedness.

"We've been nightclubbing," Kitty laughed. "There's this great little dinner theater downtown, and I don't think I've ever laughed so much in my life. The players were just fantastic!"

"Hawke not home?" Randy asked.

Siri shook her head. "He went off somewhere with Nita."

Kitty stopped in her tracks and the smile left her face. "Nita came here?" she asked.

"This afternoon. Hawke said not to expect him until late," Siri told her with a forced smile. "Don't worry, he's a grown man, he can look after himself."

"How about a drink?" Randy asked.

Siri got up out of the rocking chair and followed them inside for a nightcap. It was after midnight when they stopped talking and went to bed. But Siri lay awake involuntarily until she heard the sound of a car coming up the driveway. When she glanced at the clock, it was three in the morning. And in spite of all her efforts, she listened intently for Hawke's footsteps coming up the stairs, slowly passing her room, before she could let herself go to sleep.

The Hallers decided to spend a few more days in Charleston with Kitty's people, so Siri and Hawke flew back to Atlanta alone. She'd barely spoken to him since their late breakfast at Graystone, instead sharing her bits of conversation with the Hallers and Mrs. Simms, while Hawke sat brooding in his chair.

He unloaded their luggage from the plane and led the way quietly to the parking lot where he'd left the black Mercedes parked when they departed for Panama City. He put the suitcases in the trunk before he unlocked the car doors and turned to Siri. He looked unusually tired, and his eyes were bloodshot, as if he hadn't had any sleep at all—which, Siri thought angrily, had probably been the case.

"Would you like to have a cup of coffee before we leave?" he asked with a stranger's cool politeness.

The temptation was terrible, to spend just a few more minutes alone with him, talking to him, looking at him. It would never again be as intimate between them as it had been during those days on the beach and in Charleston. But she believed in quick, clean breaks, not painful little cuts, so she shook her head.

"Thanks, anyway," she replied with equal politeness and a strained smile, "but I'd better get home and call Bill. What can I tell him about a release date for the information you've given me on the Devolg murder?"

"Give me a day or two," he replied. "I'll send word to you by Jared."

"All right," she agreed.

As she slid into the passenger seat, she

realized what he was telling her. *When we get to Atlanta, I'm going to walk away from you and never look back.* Figuratively speaking, he'd just done that.

"Well, when then?" Bill Daeton was growling at her in his office. "My God, Siri, it's been days. I can't wait forever! Do you realize how much it cost us in expenses and your salary to send you on that trip?"

"By the time you deduct it off the paper's taxes," she replied calmly, "probably about thirty-two cents."

"Oh, hell," he grumbled, turning toward the window with his hands jammed in his pockets. "Have you heard from Hawke at all?"

"Not yet," she replied, feeling the pain of having to admit it. "He said he'd let me know, and he doesn't go back on his promises. If you'll remember," she added, "I didn't want to go on the trip in the first place."

"Don't remind me." He turned back. "I'll give you until tomorrow to convince him to let you release that information. If he puts us off any longer, we'll run it anyway."

"Oh, no, we won't," she replied curtly. "I gave my word, and I'm not going back on it for you, this paper, or anything else!"

"It's your word, or the flower show circuit," he said firmly.

"I told you before, I like flowers." She stood up. "I'll see what I can do. But no promises."

"You haven't been the same since you got back from the trip," he said quietly. "Want a day off?"

She gaped at him. "I haven't changed," she protested.

"You did that opinion poll for me yesterday without an argument," he replied with a kindly smile. "That's when I knew something was wrong."

She shrugged with a smile. "I just got my feet wet, that's all."

"Keep your shoes on next time."

"You can bet on it."

Nine

Jared wasn't looking well. She watched him at the supper table, really seeing him for the first time since she'd been home. He was pale and quiet, and it wasn't like him not to make conversation.

"Don't you feel well, Dad?" she asked with more than a trace of concern on her face.

"Not very," he admitted with a wan smile. "I don't know what's wrong with me. A little stomach upset, I suppose. Too much restaurant fare while you were gone.'' His amber eyes held hers. ''Siri, what happened on that trip?''

She shrugged, hoping the turmoil inside her didn't show. ''Nothing noteworthy. We had a very good time.''

''No, you didn't. You look like death standing up, and Hawke's in a shell dynamite couldn't blow him out of.'' He studied her thin face. ''You found out how you felt, didn't you?''

She nodded weakly.

''Did Hawke?''

''Your esteemed colleague revived an old flame,'' she murmured. ''A girl he was engaged to years ago. They were out until three in the morning.''

''That's very interesting,'' Jared said. ''Because when I asked him why he looked so haggard the afternoon you two came home, he said he'd been in a bar half the night getting plastered.''

She blinked hard at him. "Hawke? Drunk? I can't picture him that way."

"He was the portrait of a man after the night before." Jared smiled.

Siri picked up her cup and sipped the hot, black coffee. "Nita must have really gotten to him."

"Something sure did. But Hawke doesn't seem the kind of man to hold a torch for a woman who stabbed him in the back now, does he?" he asked.

She sighed, putting her cup down and sliding her chair out from under the table. "I'm going to have a glass of sherry. How about you?" she asked with a smile, ignoring the question.

He sighed. "I give up. You can ruin your own life without any help from me, I guess," he grinned. "All right, I'd love a...oh, my God!" he groaned.

He grabbed his chest and, white as a sheet, keeled over onto the soft carpet. Siri ran to him, dropping down beside him with a terrible apprehension, as she saw his labored breathing and the pain in his face. Without a word, she made a dash for the phone and called an ambulance.

The waiting was the worst part. Emergency rooms were always crowded, and full of doctors, nurses and aides who never seemed to know anything about any particular patient. Especially when it came to answering questions about a family member.

Siri sat huddled between a nervous expectant father and an old woman waiting for news of her son who'd been involved in a motorcycle accident. It seemed like hours before Dr. Swandon finally came out long enough to tell her that Jared was going to live. "It was luckily just a light heart attack," he told her. "He'll be all right. Go on home, Siri, you can see him in the morning. He isn't going anywhere."

He patted her on the head as if she

were still the child he'd delivered so
many years ago, and sent her home with
a couple of tranquilizers that he made her
promise to take at bedtime.

The house was so quiet. So quiet, without Jared in it. She tried to watch television, but it didn't take her mind off
what had happened. Oh, God, if she just
had someone to talk to, a shoulder to cry
on.

The sudden jangle of the telephone interrupted her, as if in answer to a prayer.
Maybe it would be Marty, or even Mark,
whom she hadn't heard from since she'd
been home. Right now, she'd have welcomed a phone call from the devil.

She lifted the receiver. "Hello?"

"Siri?" It was Hawke's deep, slow
voice. "I need to speak to Jared."

Hawke! She fought back a surge of
tears. If only he were here, and he cared,
and he'd hold her while she cried....

"He's not here, Hawke," she managed
in a husky whisper.

"All right, I don't have time to track him down. Tell him the Maloxx family decided to settle out of court," he told her curtly, as if he couldn't wait to get off the phone. "And if you want to start getting your story written, I'll probably be able to let you release it by tomorrow afternoon. Davy's sister goes on the stand in the morning. Have your court reporter check with me when court recesses. Goodnight."

The dial tone replaced his voice abruptly. She stood there blankly holding the receiver. Now, it seemed, he couldn't even bear the sound of her voice over the telephone, much less the sight of her.

She put the receiver back down. "Goodnight," she whispered, and burst into tears.

She got up after a sleepless night, feeling somehow more secure in the morning, with daylight outside instead of darkness. She wrapped a thick terry cloth robe around her gown and made herself a cup of coffee in the kitchen. The phone rang as she passed it, and she lifted the receiver automatically. It was Nadine, telling her to remind Jared about his court case that morning out of county. Siri told her as gently as she could about the heart attack, and asked her to contact the judge and let him know, too. Nadine promised to do that, and to go and see him as soon as she could. If Siri had ever wondered how deep the woman's emotions were involved with her father, the tremor in Nadine's normally calm voice told her. She went into the kitchen and made a pot of strong coffee.

Numbly, she sat drinking it, half-heartedly munching on a piece of toast as she tried to organize the day in her mind. The first order of business was to get to the hospital during visiting hours.

The sound of the doorbell disturbed her. She put down the cup of coffee and went to answer it, puzzling at who could be calling at that unholy hour of the morning.

She opened the door and felt her heart skip a beat as she saw Hawke standing there, grim and noticeably disturbed. His eyes swept over her drawn appearance; her tousled blond hair, the flushed freshness of her complexion without makeup, the wide amber eyes that were slightly bloodshot.

"Why the hell didn't you tell me Jared was in the hospital?" he asked tautly. "My God, I'd have been over here like a shot!"

Tears welled in her eyes. "I'm all right," she whispered.

"I can see that." He came in, shutting the door firmly behind him, and pulled her roughly into his arms, cradling her, crushing her against his big body, rocking her slowly from side to side as the tears rushed hot and wet down her cheeks.

"Hawke," she whispered against his

chest, nestled like a frightened child in his big, comforting arms. "Oh, Hawke, I needed you," she murmured weakly.

His arms tightened painfully. "You might have told me that last night when I called."

"I didn't think you wanted to be bothered with me," she said miserably. "In Charleston, you said...you said you wouldn't look back...."

"Oh, God, don't," he whispered into her soft hair. "I didn't mean for you to try and close every damned door between us."

"It sounded like it."

His arms shifted protectively. "I'll always come if you need me, Siri. At least let me take care of you when I can." She felt his lips brushing her hair. "How bad is Jared?"

"The doctor said it was a light heart attack. He'll be all right, but he's going to have to take it easy for a while," she murmured.

"In other words," Hawke said, "we'll have to tie him to a bedpost for the next few weeks."

"That's exactly right." She pulled away, wiping at her eyes with the lapel of her cream-colored robe. "Would you like some coffee and half a piece of toast?"

His eyes caressed her softly flushed face, the slightly tremulous curve of her pink mouth. "Why only half a piece?"

She smiled with a little of her old sauciness. "Because all I had in the house was one piece of bread, and I've eaten half of it."

"I think I'll pass on the toast," he chuckled softly.

"Afraid of germs?" she teased, turning to start back into the kitchen.

"As many times as I've kissed you, little girl, I think it's damned late to worry about it. Don't you?" he asked.

She was glad he couldn't see her face.

She let him into the kitchen and poured him a cup of coffee.

"I could scramble you an egg, or fix you some cereal," she offered, setting the hot coffee in front of him at the table. "Have you had any breakfast at all?"

He sat down, his eyes intent and quiet as she sank down in a chair across from him. "I rarely eat breakfast, honey," he said quietly. "Most mornings, I make do with coffee. Finish your toast."

She picked up the cold, stiff bread and studied it distastefully. "I'm really not very hungry."

He eyed the toast with a raised eyebrow. "I don't blame you."

"What time do you have to be in court?" she asked.

"In," he studied his watch, "forty-five minutes. I can drop you off at the hospital if you don't need your own car."

She smiled wanly. "I have to have it. I've got an interview with a senatorial candidate downtown at ten."

"That won't give you any time at all to spend with Jared," he remarked as he sipped the coffee.

"I know." She studied him, noting how handsome he looked in the dark gray suit and elegant, sky-blue silk tie. The silver at his temples only emphasized an attractiveness and masculinity that made music in her mind.

"You're staring again," he said softly.

"I can't help it," she murmured, dropping her eyes to her cup. "You're good to look at," she said in a bare whisper, admitting it at last.

"So are you, little one," he replied, his eyes sweeping over her. "I've never seen a woman who looked so pretty first thing in the morning."

"I'll bet you've seen plenty," she remarked.

"Siri."

She looked up involuntarily to meet his dark, level gaze.

"I didn't take Nita to bed," he told her bluntly.

She blushed like a nervous teenager. "I didn't ask you."

"I know. But it was in your eyes the next morning." His eyes brushed her mouth. "Maybe someday I'll be able to explain to you why I went with her. Right now, I don't even want to try."

"You don't owe me any explanations," she said coolly.

"Don't sit there with that damned cold look on your face and spout pride at me," he growled harshly. "I haven't forgotten how you were with me that night on the porch, and I damned well know jealousy when I see it!"

She closed her eyes on the embarrassment. She couldn't deny it, but she hated having it thrown at her like that.

"Oh, hell," he sighed heavily, "you make me feel like a damned adolescent. I can't even talk to you." He finished his coffee and stood up. "I've got to get downtown to court. Are you going to be home tonight, or has Holland come crawling back?''

She looked up at him with a frozen expression. ''I...I haven't seen him lately.''

His stormy eyes calmed a little. ''We've got to talk. I've spent one of the most miserable weeks of my life looking backwards. We've got to settle this thing between us, Siri.''

Her jaw clenched. ''I won't sleep with you,'' she said tightly.

He gave her a slow, calculating look and smiled lazily down at her. ''We'll talk about it tonight,'' he said gently.

''I...I may not be home....'' she whispered.

He moved closer, leaning down to put his mouth against hers in a kiss so slow, so tenderly thorough, that tears formed in her eyes at the beauty of it.

He raised his head, his eyes looking straight into hers, reading the turmoil in them. "You belong to me," he said quietly. "We'll talk about that, too."

He started toward the door.

"What about those seventeen years you were so worried about?" she asked in a dazed, choked whisper.

He leaned against the door facing, and his eyes held hers, dark and glowing. "Do you remember what I told you that day in Kebo's, Siri?" he asked. "That if I wanted you, the age difference wouldn't make a damned bit of difference to either one of us?"

She nodded, feeling a surge of light that burst with warm colors all through her body, as she returned that intent look.

"I want you, baby," he said softly.

Her lips parted under the force of her breath, the pounding of her heart, and she wanted to ask him if it was only a physical desire, if he cared... But before she could sort out her whirling mind, he turned and went out the door.

* * *

Jared was pale, and a little drowsy from medication, but he smiled when she came and sat by his bed. He held her hand with a firm, warm grip.

"I'm still alive, in case you wondered," he teased weakly.

"I did, actually," she returned. "I wish you'd told me you weren't well. I'd have made you see a doctor."

"That," he replied smugly, "is exactly why I wouldn't tell you."

"Incorrigible man," she grumbled.

"I'll mend, Siri," he promised. "Nadine came to see me a few minutes before you got here," he added with a grin. "Hysterical. Absolutely hysterical."

"You heartless thing, how can you smile about it like that?" she asked incredulously.

"A woman doesn't get hysterical over a man unless she cares about him," he replied. He crossed his arms behind his head with a lazy smile. "You know, I just may marry that woman."

"Finally, you've come to your senses!" Siri laughed. "I wondered if you'd ever wake up and realize what a jewel she was."

His eyebrows went up. "You approve?"

"I couldn't approve more. You know I love Nadine."

"I've been lonely since your mother died," he added softly. "Nadine's been a shot in the arm. She's attractive, and good company...."

"And she loves you to distraction," Siri finished, with a quiet smile.

He eyed her closely. "The way you love Hawke?" he asked.

She dropped her eyes to her folded hands. "I must be awfully transparent," she murmured.

"So is he," he said enigmatically. "Or don't you know yet how he feels?"

"He wants me," she said quietly.

"You really are blind if that's all you think it is," Jared told her flatly. "My gosh, he's so jealous of you he can't see straight! He has been for years, and you've never even noticed it."

"Jealous...of me?" she asked, staggered by this new insight.

"Murderously. Siri, hadn't you ever wondered why he lost his temper every time you mentioned Holland's name?"

That hadn't occurred to her before, but a lot of things were just beginning to make sense. And for the first time, she felt a sense of hope.

She finished her political interview and broke for lunch, then she went back to the office and wrote it amid a hundred interruptions. She turned it in, started on the Devolg story, working from memory and notes, and finally tracked down the court reporter to ask what information he'd gotten from Hawke.

"Two words," he told her with a grin.

"'Go ahead.' He cut the Megars girl into fish bait on the stand. She confessed to the murder five minutes after he started on her. Whew,'' he exclaimed, "I hope I never have to face that man in a courtroom. My God, I've never watched anyone that coldly efficient with words!''

Or that ruthless. He didn't say it, but she read it in his face. She knew better than most people just how ruthless her father's partner could be, how single minded. What Hawke wanted, he got. And now, he wanted Siri.... The thought made her shudder. How was she going to go about resisting him when he was suddenly her whole world? Loving him as she did would make denying that love next to impossible.

She'd just walked into Bill's office to hand him her copy. It was late afternoon, darkness lowering on the city and she'd taken her sweet time with the story because of interruptions, like returning phone calls or chasing down tacky little facts for verification. Nearly dark, nearly quitting time, and she was afraid to go home. It was almost funny.

Bill was on the phone, motioning to her to wait as he wound up the conversation. He put down the receiver roughly.

"Is anyone out there with a camera?" he asked her, gesturing toward the newsroom.

"No," she replied, "most of the day people have gone home. Why?"

"Grab your equipment and get out to Browmner Apartments," he said, "and hurry. The whole place is going up in smoke. I've got Sandy on the scene to get the story. I just need some shots. How about it?"

"I'm on my way," she agreed quickly.

She grabbed her camera and accessories and ran out to her car. She'd be late getting home for sure now. Maybe Hawke would get discouraged and she could put off the showdown until a safer time.

* * *

The two-story apartment building was totally immersed in flames by the time she got there. The county fire department had two engines on the scene, and another pulled up about the same time Siri did. Hoses and firemen in turnout gear were everywhere, and the smell of smoke was thick, pungent, and vaguely nauseating.

Residents of the complex were outside in various states of dress, watching the orange flames shooting up into the darkening sky, watching the firemen hold the pressure hoses as they shot water into the building.

Unconsciously, Siri looked for the assistant fire chief. He was new on the job, and she'd known him for several years, ever since he'd started out with the local civil defense unit as a volunteer rescue worker. Herman Jolley was a dedicated fireman, and he'd had to earn the respect of the other men on the detail. He'd done that quite successfully in only six months.

Her sharp eyes focused on his tall, thin body in the metallic turnout gear that protected the firemen from the unbearable temperatures they encountered. He was right at the front entrance, just emerging from the blazing complex with a small child held tightly in his arms. It was a perfect shot, and Siri moved quickly toward him with the camera raised, pushing her trailing scarf out of the way as she concentrated on the shot. She was clicking away when a voice shouted her name, and the thick smoke suddenly surged into her nostrils as if she were standing in the flames. A rough hand caught her, ripping the scarf form her neck, beating at her back.

She whirled in time to see the scarf dissolve in flames on its way to the ground, and blinked confusedly at one of the firemen she knew who was glowering at her.

"You crazy woman," he grumbled, "don't you know better than to ease too close to a burning building in a chiffon scarf?''

''You tell her, Smitty,'' Jolley seconded, moving in with a blackened face. ''Siri, we've told you about that before. The picture isn't worth your life, is it?''

''I'll be damned if I know how her mind works,'' came a deep, husky, very angry voice over her shoulder.

She turned and found Hawke standing there with Sandy Cudor at his side. He reached out and snatched the camera from her hands, giving it to Sandy.

''Take that to Bill Daeton,'' he told the young man. ''And tell him not to expect Siri in the morning,'' he added with blazing, dangerous eyes. ''What the hell was she doing, Herman?'' he asked Jolley.

''Trying for a prize winning shot,'' Jolley told him with a grin. ''Hit her once for me, will you? I don't like most reporters, but I'd like to see this one live a bit longer. Excuse me, folks, I think the

fire's waiting for me to come put it out.
These fatheads aren't making much head-
way.''

Jolley sauntered back off with his men,
and Hawke glared down at Siri with compressed lips.

''If you knew what I felt when I got
here and saw that scarf burning...'' He
caught her wrist with a hurtful, steely grip.
''You damned little fool, this is the last
time. The last time, Siri! From now on,
Daeton's going to put you on the meeting
circuit, or something safe!''

The anger was laced with caring, and
she heard that note in his dark voice.
''But, it's my job...''

''Not anymore,'' he said flatly. ''I'm
not risking you again.''

''You don't own me, Hawke!'' she protested.

''The hell I don't,'' he replied, jerking
her face up to his.

She looked into those glittering, dark
eyes and couldn't look away. It wasn't an-

ger that made them glow like that, but, what was it? Her fingers lifted to his hard, set face, lightly touching his profile and the chiseled line of his mouth, while around them there were the sounds and smells of the burning building, the angry voices, and the whirr of machinery.

"If you go on touching me like that," he said gently, "I'm going to have to do something about it."

"Oh..." She dropped her fingers to his jacket, and her eyes along with them. "I'm sorry."

"I'm not, Siri," he said quietly. "Let's get out of here."

She followed him meekly to his Mercedes. "What about my car?" she asked, as he put her in on the passenger side.

"I'll have it delivered back to your house," he said tightly. "Right now, I've got bigger things on my mind than cars."

They rode in silence back to Siri's house. He pulled up at the steps and escorted her inside. She took off her sweater and went to the bar in the living room, still a little shaken by her experience with the fire.

"Would you like a drink?" she asked quietly.

He took off his jacket and tie wearily, and loosened the top buttons of his shirt. He sat down heavily on the sofa and studied her in a blazing silence.

"You could have refused that assignment," he said, ignoring her question. "Were you afraid of coming home, Siri?"

She poured herself a small glass of sherry and sipped it nervously. "Of course not!" she said quickly.

"You're too pale by far, little girl," he remarked, "and thinner. Haven't you been sleeping?"

"I...I sleep fine."

"Well, I sure as hell don't," he said flatly, his eyes narrowing to glittering slits as they swept over her. "I've forgotten what it was like to sleep. Or enjoy a meal. Or watch television. Or any of the other mundane things I used to indulge in before you turned my life upside down.''

She stared at him uncomprehendingly.

''Do you want to know why I got into that car with Nita?'' he demanded angrily, ''when I could barely stand the sight of the two-timing little backstabber? I wanted to show you that those few kisses I'd given you didn't mean anything. That I could walk away from you any damned time I pleased. And I proved it.'' He sighed wearily. ''I sat in a bar until two-thirty in the morning and had to hire a cab to drive me home. I barely made it to my bed before I passed out.''

''I've never known you to drink like that,'' she said quietly.

He looked up and met her searching gaze squarely.

''You've never known me at all, Siri,'' he told her in a deep, hushed tone, ''because you've been afraid to get that close. And I've wanted you so much, for so long, that I feel as if I've had an arm ripped off.''

She finished her sherry and set the glass down on the slick finish of the padded bar. ''Wanting doesn't last, Hawke,'' she said shakily.

''Come here and prove that to me,'' he said roughly.

''What would it prove?'' she asked.

''That when I touch you, we make the sweetest fire this side of heaven together,'' he replied gently. ''That you want me every bit as much as I want you. That we're in love, Siri.''

Her eyes widened, her lips parted with a note of shock. Had she heard him right? He got up leisurely and reached her in two long strides to pull her body against the length of his, holding her close with two big arms.

''You heard me,'' he said as he bent

his head. "Oh, God, I do love you so…!"

He kissed her with an aching tenderness, a fierce soft tasting that brought a muted whisper from her soft mouth. She reached up to hold him, believing it at last, drowning in the magic of loving and being loved. Tears welled in her eyes, and even as she wept, she wanted to laugh, and cry, and shout her happiness to the world.

He drew back a breath to look at her, and everything he felt was there in his face, in his eyes. The days of pretending were finished.

"I love you," she whispered, testing the words, weighing them, making her own golden chains of them.

"I know." He brushed a stray lock of blond hair away from her flushed cheek. "I knew that day on the beach in Panama City when I held you pinned to the sand and felt your heart bursting under me while I kissed you. You may not remember exactly how you kissed me back, but I went around in a haze for the next week remembering it. You little witch, you left marks on my shoulders that haunted me every time I saw them in the mirror. That was when I had to admit to myself all you mean to me." He smiled down at her. "From that small step down, it was a quick, hard fall to the bottom. I took the Hallers to Charleston in self-defense. I had to have a buffer between us or there wouldn't have been any stopping me. It took every ounce of willpower I had to keep my hands off you."

"I thought you were still carrying a torch for Nita," she admitted, "and I was afraid to let myself feel anything deeper than affection. I wanted to run."

"So did I," he mused. "And I tried. I thought I could walk away from you and live." He sighed heavily, wrapping her closer to press a hard, rough kiss on her mouth. "I hope you like children," he murmured. "I want a son."

She smiled up at him. "Then you'll have to marry me."

"Blackmail?" he whispered huskily, brushing his hard, warm mouth tantalizingly against hers.

"Uh huh," she agreed softly. "So sue me."

"I've got something better in mind...." And he bent his head, passionately kissing her in a loving embrace that meant forever.

*   *   *   *   *

magazine

♥─────────────────────────── **quizzes**

Is he the one? What kind of lover are you? Visit the **Quizzes** area to find out!

♥─────────────────────── **recipes for romance**

Get scrumptious meal ideas with our **Recipes for Romance**.

♥───────────────────────── **romantic movies**

Peek at the **Romantic Movies** area to find Top 10 Flicks about First Love, ten Supersexy Movies, and more.

♥────────────────────────────── **royal romance**

Get the latest scoop on your favorite royals in **Royal Romance**.

♥──────────────────────────────────── **games**

Check out the **Games** pages to find a ton of interactive romantic fun!

♥───────────────────────── **romantic travel**

In need of a romantic rendezvous? Visit the **Romantic Travel** section for articles and guides.

♥─────────────────────────────── **lovescopes**

Are you two compatible? Click your way to the **Lovescopes** area to find out now!

Silhouette —

where love comes alive—online...

Visit us online at
www.eHarlequin.com